SUMMERS' REDEMPTION

The Hunters Trilogy: Book 3

SARA J. BERNHARDT

Lavish
Publishing LLC

This book is a work of fiction. The characters, incidents, and dialogue are drawn from the author's imagination and are not to be construed as real. Any resemblance to actual events or persons, living or dead, is entirely coincidental.

SUMMERS' REDEMPTION - Copyright 2018 ©

First Edition

The Hunter's Trilogy – Book 3

All Rights Reserved

Published in the United States by Lavish Publishing, LLC, Midland, Texas

Paperback edition

ISBN: 9781944985547

Cover Design by: WYCKED INK

Cover Images: ADOBE STOCK

www.LavishPublishing.com

Contents

For my Adam

Chapter One

"JANE?" my mother called, opening my bedroom door a crack.

"You can come in," I answered.

She opened the door the rest of the way and stepped into my bedroom. Her dark hair was up in a tight bun, and she had a strange, forced smile on her face. I closed the book I was reading, "Selected Works of Charles Dickens," for the third time. My mother just stared at me without saying a word. Her face seemed troubled—like there was something she wanted to say but didn't know how.

"You need something?" I asked, smiling a little.

"Uh...where's Becky?"

I pointed behind me, chuckling. "Bathroom, taking her third shower of the day."

My mom smiled flaccidly. "She's not quite adjusting to the Florida heat very well, is she?"

I laughed. "Not at all."

"I have...something," she started, "something I want to give you."

Her mood had shifted, and she seemed anxious again. This must have been what she was trying to bring herself to say. I didn't say anything as I waited for her to come clean. She approached me and handed me a leather-bound book.

"Do you remember when I asked you and Danny to keep journals?"

A little baffled, I said, "Uh...Mom, really...thanks, but I already have a diary."

"No," she retorted, shaking the book at me. "This"—she cleared her throat— "this is Danny's."

My voice became stifled and forced from my throat. "What?"

She frowned. "I haven't been able to bring myself to read it. I thought maybe you could get something out of it."

I nodded as I slowly took the journal from her hands. I felt as if it were made of glass and if I were to drop it, I would destroy everything that was left of my brother.

"Thanks," I choked out. I already felt the heat rushing to my face and the stinging in my eyes.

Becky entered the room, shattering the tension. She had a towel wrapped under her arms and a huge grin on her face.

"Hi, Carol!" she chirped.

"Hi, Becky," my mother answered, nodding her head. "You doing okay in this heat?" she asked with a light laugh.

Becky groaned. "It just doesn't get hot like this in Oregon. I feel so gross all the time. I don't know how you two have been able to stand it."

My mom shrugged. "It's not too different from California. You get used to it." She smiled. "Well, I'll leave you two alone."

"Oh my God, Jane!" Becky exclaimed. "I swear it's like I'm sweating *in* the shower."

I couldn't listen to Becky's chattering. My mind was elsewhere. My mom quietly closed the door on her way out as I stared at the journal in my hands, unable to take my eyes off it. I begged my mind to show me Danny just one more time. I felt that if I stared at the journal long enough, somehow, he would appear. I could feel myself slowly sinking down into memories of my twin, but Aidan came too, intertwined with the visions of Danny and Rudy. I forgot where I was for long moments, so lost in my thoughts.

"Jane?" I heard Becky's voice from far off. Her voice became louder as she tore me violently out of my daydreams. "Jane!"

I lightly shook my head, brushing off the lingering visions and brought my gaze to hers.

"Huh?"

"Are…you okay?" she asked me, still with a half-smile on her face.

"Uh, yeah," I said, setting the journal on the floor. "I'm fine."

"What's that?" she asked, nodding at where I dropped the book.

I shrugged my shoulders. "Nothing," I lied. "Just something my mom gave me for a diary."

She chuckled. "Oh. So what do you say?"

"About what?"

"Were you listening to me at all?" she demanded.

"Uh…sorry, Becky. No, not really."

"Okay," she started, pausing between her words playfully. "Do… you…want…to…go to the mall with me?"

I smiled, but it was completely artificial. Why did my best friend have to be so outgoing *all* the time? She *did* come all the way here to visit me. I was sure I could handle the mall just one time.

I nodded. "Sure, but I'm not buying *any* swimsuits."

She chuckled and raised her hand. "I promise."

Becky let me drive, still persistent she would never again trust herself in a car with me. I tried to focus on conversation and not drift away into my thoughts like I often did when Danny was on my mind. I slipped on my oversized sunglasses in a feeble attempt at diminishing the strong Florida sun as my car sliced through the palm frond shadows scattered along the smooth road lined with purple wildflowers.

"What kind of stores do you have here?" she asked, slightly hopping in her seat.

I laughed. "Same ones we have at home."

She frowned. "Oh. Really?"

"Well, there may be some things you haven't seen."

A huge grin reappeared on her face. "Great! I need new shoes and definitely a couple new skirts. It's just too hot for jeans."

I smiled and nodded. "July isn't supposed to be cool."

We laughed in unison, and it felt good to be connecting with Becky again. Those not so long-ago days in North Bend just didn't seem at all important anymore. With or without them, Becky and I would always be friends.

I heard a high-pitched chirp escape her mouth as she pulled out her brand new, fancy cell phone.

"Ah," she murmured. "Aaron. He's been texting me all day."

"When did you get a cell phone?" I asked over the clicking of her keypad.

"When I asked my mom for one. I guess she decided if she buys me enough things, it'll make up for her ignoring me. I think she forgets my name sometimes," she answered with a bitter smile.

I touched her hand.

Her smile faded, and she sighed. "Yeah...anyway."

I hated her tough-girl act. I wished she would actually talk to me about her mom. Ignoring it wouldn't make it go away.

"Yeah," I said, trying to get my mind off the uncomfortable thoughts. "Anyway."

"What about lunch?" she asked. "Any good Italian places nearby?"

"I'm not made of money, Becky."

"Oh, don't be crazy!" She laughed. "I've got you covered. I owe you for all the coffee from Books by the Bay anyway."

I smiled. "I miss that place."

"Me too," she sang. "A lot of good memories there. A lot of beautiful man memories...that I no longer need because I have my man. But we'll go there together soon. Okay?"

"Sounds great," I answered. "Though North Bend still makes me a bit nervous."

"You're telling me," she grunted. "After all the craziness from the past year, it's almost enough to make anyone swear off men—even *me*."

I laughed loudly. "How is Aaron by the way?"

"Oh, he's fine. Acting like he's going to die without seeing me during the summer."

I smiled. "Ah, come on. That's sweet."

"I wasn't complaining. It's good to be missed. I miss him too. I guess that's normal."

I nodded. "It is, Becky, when you actually care about someone."

She glanced at her phone again. "It's really good to be missed."

I wish I knew.

The mall wasn't as crowded as the one back home in North Bend. Of course, then I realized it was Thursday, and most normal people were at work—where I should be. I felt like getting a job was pointless. I expected to be back in North Bend before too long. I was so sick of moving.

Strolling through the mall with Becky ended up being a lot more enjoyable than I had originally thought. We spent a lot of time laughing while Becky snapped pictures with that camera she had constantly attached to her hand. After Becky was finished wasting money on over-priced name brand accessories, we stopped for lunch at a little Italian restaurant across from the mall.

"So what is it with you and your man?" she asked me, glancing at me from behind her menu.

"What are you talking about?" I asked innocently.

She dropped her menu on the table. "Oh, come *on,* Jane! It's me, and you should know I'm going to get it out of you, so let's save fifteen minutes of our lives, shall we?"

"Becky…there's nothing to 'get out of me.' Nothing is *with* me and *any* man."

She shook her head. "Liar. *You* told me he came back, remember? After that…um…whole shower thing."

I sighed, not wanting to think about it. I wanted to leave his memory behind me. Becky, however, was making that clearly impossible.

"He did," I said evenly. "Then he disappeared again."

"Oh," she murmured. "Sorry."

"It's fine," I said, taking a breath. "It's really fine. It's for the best."

I wasn't sure how much of that I believed, but the farther away Aidan was, the farther away all those terrible memories were. What was painful, however, was that along with those bad memories were a lot of wonderful memories and the bonds I had created with my friends. Those were the things I wished to keep with me but was forced to push away in order to protect myself.

It wasn't too long before our waitress brought us our food. Becky ignored her cheese tortellini, Caesar side salad, and lemon water, leaving them mostly untouched on the table, clearly more interested in talking than in her food. Rehashing this was the last thing I wanted to do right now.

"What exactly happened?" she asked.

I stabbed at my penne pasta with a fork. "You want details?"

"No, not like that. I just mean…you told me about your…*encounter* but not much else."

"Well, soon after…that…" I paused, searching for the right words to say.

"Yeah?"

I exhaled, trying to get my bearings. "He told me he had to go back to North Bend."

"Did he say why?"

I raised my eyebrows. "Does he ever?"

She shrugged. "Okay, so…?"

"So…he left. That's it."

"That's *not* it."

"It is. Becky, eat, girl," I said, pointing toward her plate with my fork.

Becky huffed and stuck a forkful of lettuce. "Jane, you just told me you made love with Aidan. You have no feelings about that at all?"

"No."

"Just because you don't want to, doesn't make it so."

"Okay," I started, "I don't know if I should have let it go that far. Yes, I love him. We've established that. But being with him has brought me nothing but pain."

"That isn't true," she said. "Your pain wasn't because of Aidan. Don't you remember? He was your comfort."

I shook my head. "I don't want to talk about this anymore. Please."

She nodded. "Okay. I guess we can head home if you want."

"If you would hurry up and eat."

She giggled and feigned a dramatic eyeroll. "Fine. Geez." She shoveled too much salad into her mouth. "Happy?" she said, the word distorted by her full mouth.

I laughed, shaking my head.

Becky ended up finishing her meal before me and sat cross-legged, tapping her fingers on the table impatiently as I ate the last of my pasta one piece at a time.

"Seriously?" she asked.

"Oh, I'm sorry. Are you in a hurry?" A deep snicker broke through my attempt at sincerity, and I burst out laughing.

"You're such a dork," she said, joining in with my laughter. "Come on. Let's go."

Chapter Two

AS WE HEADED out of the restaurant, I wasn't sure at first if I heard what I thought I heard. I just kept walking, picking up my pace while Becky chattered. With that one word, the heat had rushed to my cheeks, and my heart was pounding in my ears. My stomach was twisted into knots, and I felt so lightheaded I thought I was going to be sick. I heard that sound echo in my head again. There aren't words to describe the meaning of it. It was like a feeling, like a previously un-named emotion that he had personally coined *Jane*.

I knew it was my name. It was simply my name. So why did it sound like some magical utterance spoken only by *him*? It sent a resonance through my brain. I stopped in the parking lot and took a fortifying breath.

"Jane?"

My nerves screeched, and my ears were screaming at me. *Please let this be a dream. Please let this not be Aidan. Anyone but Aidan.*

Becky was instantly silenced, and she turned around even before I did, nudging me in the shoulder. I took another deep breath, closing my eyes, and turned around. I kept my eyes shut for a moment before being able to open them. When I did, my senses were assaulted with more than what I was seeing but also with a flood of memories and tangled emotions.

I tried to speak. I really did. But his beauty left me speechless as it always had. He took one long stride toward me and pulled me into his arms. His sudden embrace was almost my undoing. I tried to move away, but I couldn't. I didn't return his touch but couldn't bring myself to push him away. His arms were strong yet gentle at the same time. My memory flashed with the visions of the dark days in North Bend when his embrace was my only comfort.

"Sorry I took so long." He moved away from me with a beautiful, wide grin on his face. "I missed you."

I still couldn't say anything.

"Are you all right?"

I cleared my throat. "H-hi, Aidan."

"Um…hi, Jane. What's going on? What's wrong?"

Oh, if only I could tell him. "Nothing," I lied. "Nothing. I'm fine. You just surprised me."

"I told you I was coming back." He still sounded happy and casual.

"Oh, *did* you?" Becky asked, crossing her arms and looking at me accusingly.

I shrugged my shoulders, avoiding her eyes that were seeing entirely too much of me. "When was it a good idea to believe something just because *Aidan* says it's true?"

"What can I do to get you to trust me again?" he demanded, almost peeved.

"Probably nothing!" I remarked curtly. "Becky and I have to go."

"No, you don't," Aidan snapped, reaching for my arm.

"Yes," Becky said, cutting off his path to me, "we do."

"Explain, please, because I really don't get it," Becky complained.

"There is *nothing* to *get,* okay?" I snapped.

"There definitely is, especially because of how adamant you are that there isn't."

"That doesn't even make any sense," I replied.

She laughed, instantly relaxed again. "Come on, Jane. Just talk to me about it. I know you are a private person, but I am, oh…what do they call it? Your *best* friend." She smiled at me to take the sting out of her criticism.

"Fine," I said, rounding on her. "Under one circumstance."

She raised her eyebrows in question.

"*You* have to talk to me about your mom."

"What?" she whispered, going a little pale.

"That's the deal."

She huffed. "Seriously?"

"Yes."

She sighed, resigned, and turned away from me. "Fine, but…you first."

I nodded. "I don't really know where to start."

"How about with why you were so harsh toward him? I backed you up because we're best friends and that's what we do, but I want to know why you won't follow your heart. Why you won't give it to him."

"He *broke* my heart!" I yelled. "That should be a good enough reason for anyone."

"Since when has heartbreak ever stopped you from living your life?" she asked gently. "I remember when we lost Danny, and I remember how determined you were to keep going. You even left your house to try to keep living…for yourself and for your brother's memory."

"It's not the same thing, Becky! Not even close. Danny was gone, and there was nothing I could do to change that. But Aidan lied. He lied, and he kept leaving. Not to mention that minor detail of he killed my twin! Now it's suddenly supposed to make sense for me to be with the man who killed him? Because I fell in love with him?"

"If it's like he said…it was out of compassion, Jane. Mercy."

"It's sick," I muttered. "I hate thinking about Danny as an example or a suspect of mercy."

She nodded. "I'm sorry. I know it's hard to think of, but that already happened, and Aidan did the best he could for Danny in the *past*. This is now, Jane, and Aidan loves you. He always has. And you love him just

SARA J. BERNHARDT

as much. Why can't you admit it? I can feel it every time I see you two together."

"I can—I do!" I cried. "But that's what you aren't getting. Sometimes love isn't enough. Sometimes you need more to conquer all."

"No," she whispered, touching my shoulder. "Love is *always* enough. The world bows before love."

I sighed. "You really think that Aidan and I together have some kind of power to fight the forces of evil?" I tried to laugh. "It's not a fairy tale, Becky."

"Wars have been fought and won over it before. How is your love story any different? You can still write out your happily ever after."

I did laugh then. Loud and a little hysterically, considering how *un*funny I actually found it. "What? The Grimm Brothers have nothing on your fairy tales, Becky, if that is what you really think."

"You know, I always envied you two, even knowing what I do," she started. She tried to keep her face completely blank, but I saw a strange emotion flicker across her eyes. Even when she looked away from me, I could see it taking shape. It left me wondering what she was going to say. "You had this sort of uncertain affection for each other. Though you were skeptical to trust him, you still loved like *nothing* could stop you. And nothing ever should."

I could still see this look of desperation in her eyes as if she were begging me to believe her. She was right. I hated that she was right. "What else can I say?" I muttered, blinking away my tears, fighting the break in my words and the splinters in my phrases. "It just hurts too much."

She leaned over and wrapped me in a hug. I gave up the fight and let myself cry. I was stronger when I was with Becky. Together *we* could take on the world.

She sat there rubbing my back gently until I was able to get some semblance of control and push the conversation to the back of my mind.

I moved away from her, drying my eyes with the back of my hand. I took a deep breath. "Your turn."

Her face fell, and her eyes lost that look of confidence. "I don't know how to talk about it."

Her words were frail, almost like she was losing the strength to speak.

"We made a deal," I pressed. I raised my eyebrows. "It's me, Becky. I won't judge you."

She nodded. "I know. I'm just not sure you'll understand. Even with being my best friend and all…there are things it feels like nobody could understand."

"Try me," I said, leering at her to try to lighten the mood.

She sighed heavily and gave in. I could almost feel the nervousness shaking through her.

"Okay," she said. "It feels like you've always had this perfect life."

I grunted. "Hardly!"

She smiled sadly. "You really have no idea, even with Danny…" She trailed off for a second, seemingly trying to gather her strength. "Your mom is the only mother I've ever really known."

I nodded. "I know."

"And I'm so thankful for that, Jane. I really am."

"But?"

"But"—she sighed— "she's yours…you know? She's…not *my* mom, and I feel like you have something that I have unfairly been deprived of. Like I deserve to be loved the same as you. Your mom can never love me the way she loves you."

"Oh, that isn't true at all. My mom loves you like her own."

She shook her head. "She can't, and I don't hold that against anyone, but she can't. It's just not the same. Every time I'm here with you, I love feeling like part of your family. Christmas was amazing, but at the same time, I'm often only reminded of all the things I never had."

I didn't know what to say.

"Don't get me wrong," she said. "It's not like you make me feel worse. It's because of you I'm still here."

I prepared myself to respond until her words sank in, and something hit me. "What did you say?"

"See? This is why I didn't want to talk about it."

Her head was down as if she would refuse to look at me if her life depended on it.

"Now is when you really need to talk to me," I said.

She didn't say a word, just started shaking her head back and forth.

"Look at me," I said. "I'm not going to be angry, but you need to talk about this."

She finally looked up, and tears were rolling down her cheeks, smearing up her perfectly applied makeup. What could be so terrible that my strong best friend would break down like this?

"Becky…"

She begged me. "Please—I don't want to tell you."

"I already know," I said, "so why not just let me help you through it."

"You already have," she whispered, choking on the last of her words. "I'm still here, aren't I? I didn't take the easy way out."

"That's not good enough," I said. "Let me see."

"See what?"

"Becky, you know what."

She took a deep breath and held it as her shaking hands hesitantly pulled down the waist band of her skirt, showing me tiny lines all along the front of her thighs and hips. The cuts looked like they had been shallow, but nonetheless—they were there, and there were many.

"They have mostly disappeared," she said.

"I would have never noticed."

"That was the point," she answered. "I knew it was stupid, Jane. But I needed it, for so long. I needed that control, that temporary rush that it brought. She never made me feel like I was there, like I was even alive. This did. The pain let me know I am human, that I can feel and bleed like everyone else. But you're the one who kept them away from my wrists."

"All of this…and all these years. You never told me?"

"I couldn't," she said, sobbing. "Can you see why I envy you now? You have a mother who adores you and a man who will kill to protect you, and you aren't even acknowledging it. This helped me cope."

"I could have helped."

She shook her head. "Not any other way than you already were."

I sighed and dropped my gaze.

"You think terribly of me now, don't you?"

I instantly shot my gaze back to her. "God, Becky, not at all!" I exclaimed. "It's just that I always envied your happiness and your confidence. It would hurt me to know that none of that is real."

"It is real," she said, "but only when I am hanging out with you or Aaron. We all have masks, Jane, ones we can exchange from day to day. That is one that I use a lot. But yours…I can't even see through yours all the time."

I tried to smile. "And your mom?"

She huffed. "Please! She's so busy with her boyfriends. If I ask her for something, she'll give it to me. I guess she thinks that way, I'll stop asking. Technically, she doesn't have to pay for it anyway. She always has some new man taking care of her."

"You're still her daughter."

She shrugged. "Yeah, well, I wasn't exactly planned. I was an accident, remember? A mistake."

"Don't call yourself that," I said. "You know I hate it."

"Not my words, Jane."

"It doesn't matter," I said. "She's making a bigger mistake by not taking care of you. You being born was not your fault, and your mom should have still been happy to have you. She has *no* idea how lucky she is."

"Lucky?" She almost laughed at that.

"Any mother would love to have a daughter like you. You're driven, you make everyone around you smile, and you're beautiful and smart. You're strong and independent! I envy that."

She smiled tentatively. "Really?"

"Really. And if your mom can't see that…then she's the one missing out on things. She's the one being deprived of things. Not you."

She nodded. "And you really believe this?"

"Of course."

She smiled again and bowed her head. I could hear the tears behind her words again. "That's why *you're* my family."

15

It was difficult to leave Becky alone after that. I knew she didn't want to talk about it, but it felt to me like I *could* help even if she didn't believe I could. I was considerably hurt in a way that she felt she had to keep something like that from me. Tears were still moistening her eyes when she looked at me.

"What?" she asked. "Are you mad?"

"Becky, please stop thinking I'm mad," I answered. "I already told you I'm not mad at you. I just feel a little hurt that you didn't think you could trust me."

She sighed. "It isn't like that."

"Then what is it 'like'?"

"I didn't want to worry you, okay?"

I smiled. "I worry anyway."

She mirrored my smile and nodded. "Exactly. That's my point. I didn't want to add to your worry. Worrying is one thing you're very good at."

"Yeah, the only thing," I said, chuckling. "Maybe you should let me indulge a little in my one talent."

She laughed. "Sure. Really though, Jane—anything else—I promise to tell you. I won't keep anything from you again. No more secrets?"

I nodded. "No more secrets. Meaning I do have something to say to you…about Aidan."

She instantly perked up, smiling. "Really?" she squealed. "Tell me!"

"I love him."

"Duh!" She laughed. "What else?"

"No, I mean…" I paused, trying to think of the right words, the most honest words. "I mean…I love him, I trust him, I forgive him, and I understand him. I want him more than anything, and I'm driving myself half insane trying to push him away."

"I know," she said calmly, sounding like she really did know. "But, Jane…Danny wants you to be happy. I believe that."

"I don't know if I do," I answered. "I mean…of course he wants me to be *happy*. I'm just not sure he wants me to be happy with Aidan."

She nodded. "Give it some time. Maybe something will change."

"While on the topic of change," I said, holding out my hand, "give me your knife."

She slapped my hand in a low five where I held it out. "Pardon?"

"Come on, Becky," I urged, shaking my hand at her. "You have pepper spray—give me the pocket knife."

"Don't you trust me?" she asked, her eyes going hard and her posture turning defensive.

"I love you," I said, "so I'm helping you."

She sighed.

"It'll give me some peace of mind," I said. "Please?"

She grumbled. "Fine, but you'd better not lose it."

She reached into her purse and handed me her old-fashioned pocket knife.

"The blade on this is too big anyway," I murmured.

She shrugged. "No such thing. So…let's do dinner," she announced, as if the conversation hadn't even happened. Maybe she was trying to end the tension.

I laughed. "All right, Becky. Dinner."

Chapter Three

TO HANG OUT, just be together as friends so I can show you how easy it is to be with me.

Being the idiot that I was, I had agreed to that. Not that it was really that bad. In fact, that's what had made it so terrible—the fact that it went so well. I didn't want him to be right. I wanted him to be bad, to be— evil. I wanted him to be something, anything that would make it easier for me to hate him. At the same time, how could I be sure that that's what Danny would have wanted—all this struggling? Aidan could be completely insufferable sometimes, but that usually only occurred when he happened to be right about things I turned myself blue arguing over. It was already a challenge to trust him on anything, and then for him to be right in all his assumptions left me even more confused.

I leaned back against the couch, ignoring the annoying late-night sitcom, which was hardly even audible through the turned down volume. I felt my mind descending into memory, which was really not what I wanted, but it was nearly impossible to avoid, and I was far too tired to try.

· · ·

"It's my treat," he said. "Really. I'm the one who begged you to come with me."

I tried to smile, tried to pretend it wasn't already awkward. Why did it have to be here? Why did it have to be just like the place we met? This wasn't the only place with good coffee, was it? It was like "Happy Days" where there was only one burger place around. It was bigger than Books by the Bay, and there were computers lined up against the walls, but the neatly stacked bookshelves with the tight, cramped aisles and the little, round coffee tables were all too similar. I just sat silently, trying not to focus on my surroundings; it would only stir up more memories—memories that I had spent countless hours trying to repress.

"Would you at least look at me?" he asked with harsh insist behind his words.

I looked up into his eyes, which were once again that piercing green color I had fallen so in love with. He smiled at me, probably being fully aware that my vitality would deteriorate as soon as he flashed me a glimpse of his beauty.

"There," he said. "Now we can actually talk."

I nodded feebly, unable to protest.

"How's your mom's place working out?"

"Come on, Aidan," I spat, slightly chuckling but certainly not from amusement. "Is that the best you can do?"

He shrugged, still with a smirk. "I just want to talk about something other than the same things we've been talking about."

"I know. I don't want to talk about that either."

"I don't think there is much else to say on the matter."

I nodded. "You're right. There isn't."

He sighed and opened his mouth to speak, but I interrupted.

"How old are you, Aidan?" I asked calmly.

"I told you," he answered.

"Yes, but was it true?"

He nodded and dropped his gaze. "I turned twenty-one last March."

I sighed, almost gasped. Twenty. He was a very good actor, and—as I was already aware—an amazing liar.

"It doesn't make sense."

"Doesn't it?" he pressed. "Doesn't it make sense to completely re-create me? Abraham needed me to be his weapon, his tool. The only way he could do that would be to build me himself to be everything he needed. On top of all of that, my identity needed to be kept a secret."

"So what ever happened to Clement Thortan?" I almost thought I saw him shudder at the sound of his true name—his past.

"As far as record says, he doesn't exist."

"Friends and family?"

He shook his head. "There are none."

"I guess that made it easy."

He shook his head again. "I'm more capable than you think of making someone disappear." He raised his eyebrows.

I bowed my head, unable to look at him again.

"I'm sorry," he said. "I can't be normal, Jane, not as normal as you want me to be."

"I don't want you to be normal," I said, slowly bringing my gaze back to his. "I just want you to be good."

"I told you everything. There is nothing else that isn't in plain view for you now. Hold it against me if you want to. I don't care. Just please let yourself find a way to forgive me. Please try to find a way to look at me the way you used to."

His eyebrows furrowed, and he had this look of complete and utter defeat littered in his features. It hurt me to see him look so helpless and miserable.

I shook my head. "I'm trying."

"No, you aren't."

"Okay," I answered. "I'm trying not *to. It's taking every ounce of will power I possess to not hurl myself over this table and into your arms. Is that what you wanted to hear?"*

He smiled. "Something like that."

I cringed. "Damn, Aidan, you aren't making this very easy."

"I disagree," he said with that familiar childlike tone in his voice. "I think I am making it very simple. You are the one who's complicating things." He swiftly crossed his arms and leaned his elbows on the table

as he bent toward me. "Are we ever going to talk about that day at your mom's?"

"What day?"

He tilted his head down while keeping those green eyes intently focused on me. "You know what day."

"Oh, you mean the one where you charged into the bathroom like a crazy person?"

I thought I saw a smile tug at the corners of his perfect lips. "Yes, that day."

"No," I said. "We're not going to talk about that."

"And why not?"

"Because..."

"Because?"

"Because...I don't know what it means, okay?"

"Um...I'm pretty sure what it means."

"No, you know what you want it to mean. That's not the same thing."

He leaned forward again, staring into my eyes.

I looked away from him, and he leaned closer to me. "Give in," he murmured. "Stop denying me just to prove you can."

"It isn't about that!" I hissed.

"But it can't really be all about me," he said, "because you still want me, and it can't be all about you because you are almost incapable of being selfish. So what's it about?"

"It's about Danny," I said harshly, getting up from the table and storming out.

"Jane!" he called after me. "Jane, if you want to leave, at least let me take you home."

"I'll walk."

"It isn't North Bend," he yelled. "It's too far to walk."

"Leave me alone."

"You know I can't do that!" he insisted. "Please just stay? Please?"

That sad, pleading tone made me so angry. I couldn't refuse him, and he knew it. "Fine," I said, "but if you want to show me how easy it is to be with you, then we are going to need to pretend we know almost nothing about each other."

"Okay."
We went back inside and sat back down at our original table.
"So..." he started.
"My mom's place is nice," I said with a forced smile.

I came back to the warm living room and boring sitcom. I honestly couldn't remember much of what else was said, but there was a lot of smiling, a lot of laughing, and an almost too forceful goodnight kiss that I couldn't have denied even if I wanted to. It didn't seem like there was anything wrong with loving Aidan—until the inevitable return of the North Bend memories. However, the memories weren't bad; in fact, I enjoyed looking back on our adventure and my leap of faith in him. I enjoyed the bonds I had made with the best people in the world and the stories I might later get to tell my grandchildren. So why did I want so badly to hate him just for Danny? I wanted to let go, but I just couldn't do it yet, not until I could be sure it would be right. I didn't know if I could ever be sure of that.

It was a week before I was able to even open Danny's journal. I just stared at the first page for what seemed like hours. It was a picture of us that must have been taken just before he died. I recognized the shirt he was wearing, the one I had bought him for our fourteenth birthday. He was just standing there with a huge grin on his face. I was next to him with my arms wrapped around his shoulders. My smile was thin, but the happiness was visible in my eyes. Just seeing him there made it seem like he had never really been gone in the first place. I stared at the image for so long that it almost began to look like it was moving. I blinked my eyes and turned the page. The tears were instant when I saw his adorable writing on the first blank page.

Chapter Four

DANIEL'S THOUGHTS

If I were to turn one more page, I could read those thoughts. My fingers brushed the corner of the page, but before I could bring myself to turn it, I slammed the book closed and dropped it back onto the floor beside my bed, being careful not to wake Becky. I switched off my lamp and curled up, trying to clear my mind so I could actually sleep. I didn't succeed at not thinking about Danny or what might be written in that journal. What if I were to find out things about him that I didn't want to know? What if I just wanted to remember Danny a certain way and that journal would ruin things? I did always wonder where he would sometimes go at night. He promised me he'd take me one day.

"I don't like keeping secrets from you," he had said. "I promise to explain everything to you, and someday, I will even take you with me."

I remembered the honesty in his voice. That conversation was as crisp and clear in my mind—as real as anyone could remember anything. My mind was so awake and noisy with my thoughts and memories that I couldn't even remember falling asleep. I knew I had dreamed of Danny, not because I remembered it but because of how close I felt to him when I awakened. It was a wonderful feeling, like I missed him so much less than I had before. I tried to talk to Becky, but Daniel was something already so grueling to talk about that I couldn't get the words out even to my best friend. I was noticeably depressed throughout the day and at lunch. Becky finally decided to say something.

"Why don't you just go talk to him?"

I was pulled from my thoughts and had no idea what she was talking about. "Huh?"

She chuckled halfheartedly. "Aidan."

My throat constricted as my thoughts took that rapid turn, but I regained my composure. "Oh…" I cleared my throat, trying to think of something to say. "We've talked about this, Becky," I said. "I will talk to him…when the time is right."

"Well, staring at him won't make things easier," she said, laughing. "What?"

She cocked her head to the side, and there he was. I guess when staring into space, I was actually subconsciously staring at Aidan. I sighed. *Damn.*

"Hey," he said, walking up to the table.

Becky smiled at him but didn't reply, making it impossible for me to just let them talk.

"Hi," I said, only loud enough for him to hear me.

"Are you okay?" he asked.

"Not now, Aidan," I whispered. "I'm with my friend. Call me tomorrow."

He nodded. "Sure."

Becky instantly complained about me avoiding him again.

"I'm with you right now," I said.

"You're with me all summer."

"Yeah, but right now we are out together. Me and you."

She smiled. "It's why I love you."

I groaned. "I told him to call me tomorrow," I whined, placing my face in my hands. "Why did I do that?"

She laughed. "Relax. It'll be fine."

. . .

It *was* fine, only because I didn't answer the phone. I only hoped he wouldn't come to my house. That would be a mistake on his part.

Becky was in the shower, so I decided I would try again to look through my brother's journal. After that first page, my hands were shaking. I turned the page, trying to stay calm.

July 2, 2006

I really tried to tell Jane about my work. I couldn't. Sterling agrees that it isn't best for her to know. I'm not sure Sterling is as smart as he seems to be. He's capable, and he's determined, but he often doesn't make sense. Jane is my sister. I know her better than anyone. So why does he feel he can't trust her? Perhaps I shouldn't take it so personally. Sterling is simply trying to be cautious.

I cannot take Jane with me. Not yet. She is strong and brave, but I am her brother, and protecting her is my most important job. It's my life or hers, and I will not let her die because of something I got involved in by my own choice. She isn't ready yet. She has yet to understand the ways in which our world works.

My entire body was shaking. *The ways in which the world works.* I knew those words. I had heard them before. I replayed them in my mind over and over, putting the emphasis on different words and syllables, trying to spark a memory. Nothing was working. Something wasn't right. I began thinking that maybe Danny was writing fiction...but that was wishful thinking. All I wanted was something of my brother to hold on to, and now...there was something wrong, something I had to figure out.

Chapter Five

I DON'T KNOW how many times I read this words in Danny's journal, but finally the sentence played in my head in a different voice than my own. My memory flashed with horrific images and terrifying nightmares as all the sordid memories of North Bend came raining down on me, making me feel almost sick. Those words. I knew I had heard them before. I had heard them when I was locked in a dark, dusty basement, fighting for my life beside a hanging corpse. Alex. Aidan's cult brother had talked to me about not understanding the ways in which the world works. I couldn't believe it took me so long to remember. It was something I had tried so hard to forget. That twisted mantra was a Sevren teaching, a Sevren belief. My throat constricted, and I was sobbing uncontrollably. My brother...was a Sevren.

I knew at that point I had to tell Becky. As soon as she walked out of the bathroom and back into my room, she instantly rushed to my side.

"Oh my gosh. What happened?" she yelled with obvious concern behind her words. "Are you okay?"

I shook my head. "I don't know," I said through my sobs. I fell into her chest and found myself in hysterics.

"Shh," she whispered. "Hey, you need to relax and tell me what happened. Whatever it is, we'll figure it out."

"No," I cracked. "Nobody can fix it."

I could feel her heartbeat speed up. I must have been terrifying her. I moved away from her and handed her the journal.

"I'm sorry," I said. "I wasn't able to tell you about this before. Now I am." I opened to the first page again.

"Oh my God," she mumbled. "This is…"

I nodded. "Turn the page."

She stared at me for a moment with a bewildered expression on her face. I nodded again, pressing her.

She turned the page but waited a moment before reading it. I waited for her to join my tears—but she didn't.

"Becky?" I whispered.

"I don't understand," she said.

"You don't?" I yelled. "Well, neither do I. How can anyone understand that someone like Danny could be a Sevren?"

"Whoa!" she cried, raising her hands. "Think about what you're saying, Jane!"

I didn't answer.

"This is *Danny*. We know Danny, better than anybody."

"That's why it's so hard to understand."

"No," she said. "It's impossible to believe. Someone as wonderful as Danny would *never* be a Sevren."

"Aidan was!" I yelled.

"Aidan was also lost and deceived."

"I don't know."

"Think about it, Jane."

I went through the words I had read and began to cry again.

"He died for me," I said. "He's dead because of me."

She just held me until I was able to calm myself. I tried to focus on the fact that I knew Danny and that he wasn't always that great with words. Maybe I had misunderstood; maybe I was taking things completely out of context. If I only read more—but that thought terrified me. How could I keep reading when I was so sure he was part of the one thing that destroyed my life? I didn't want to remember him as a villain. Danny was killed by The Sevren. What else could he possibly be talking about? The tears didn't stop for a long time, but Becky stayed calm and sweet like she always was. It was hard for me to lean on her and dump all my problems on her. I was usually so good at hiding my feelings and my fears, but when it came to my brother—the most important thing I had lost—it happened often that I needed her more than I realized.

Becky didn't push me to talk about the journal. She realized I needed to work things out my own way before moving forward with it. I still didn't feel like things were resolved with her, so it wasn't right to move on to me.

"Becky?" I touched her shoulder.

She turned to me.

"What's wrong?" I asked.

She was sitting on the edge of the bed, wrapped in a towel, her hair still dripping wet.

"Nothing. I was just…thinking," she said, her voice far away.

"About what?"

"Just…" Her voice trailed off.

"Your mom?"

She didn't answer, just turned away from me and nodded.

"Do you want to talk about it?"

She shrugged. "I know she and I were never really close, but…I don't know. Sometimes I just miss her. Is that stupid?"

"It's not stupid. I can understand. Maybe you can try talking to her."

She scoffed. "Right."

"Well, why not? It's worth a shot, isn't it?"

She shook her head. "No. It's not. It's not like I haven't tried that. She really hates me, Jane."

"I'm sure that isn't true."

"It doesn't matter. She's not interested in talking. I don't feel like putting myself through that anymore. I learned a long time ago that the best way to protect myself and not let my mom keep hurting me was to stop trying."

I sighed. "I know."

"I'm gonna get dressed," she said, getting up from the bed. "Let's hit a café." Her voice still sounded far away as though she weren't really there.

I nodded. "Sure."

The café was a little busy when we got there, and Becky still refused to make eye contact with me. She was completely silent on the drive over —very unlike her. I'd seen her like this before, but it had been a very long time. The last time she shut down like this was back in middle school. She was twelve, and her mom forgot her birthday—again. I didn't push. I let her sort things out on her own like she did for me. She stared into her coffee. I knew I had to say *something*.

"I like your shirt," I said.

"Stop," she muttered. She looked up at me and was smiling.

I smirked. "I actually do," I said. "Black looks good on you."

She chuckled half-heartedly. "I'm fine. I promise."

I exhaled slowly. "Long week."

"Yeah. You're telling me."

The smile in her voice eased my nerves, and I felt a little better about moving on to my own issues. It had already been a few days of me trying to ignore the haunting thought of Danny's secret life before I could think about it again. Everything I could know was in that journal. So why was it so hard to open it again?

"Now what are *you* thinking about?" Becky asked, giving me an accusing look, completely herself again.

I didn't answer.

"Aidan?" She batted her eyes.

I smacked her arm, laughing. "Danny, actually."

"Ah. He's been on my mind too. I'm dying to read the rest of his journal."

"I know, but...I'm still a little scared."

"It's Danny," she said again. "Remember that."

I sighed, reserved. "Fine. You're right."

We got up at the same time and headed home.

I opened the journal, and my hands were already shaking. I took a deep breath and turned to the next page.

July 5th, 2006

It's strange just going through the holidays with my family and friends as if everything was normal. Then returning to Sterling again and feeling like a completely different person. This double life thing isn't exactly what I had in mind. I have to protect Jane though. I have to protect Mom and Dad too. I have to keep all of them safe, and in order to do that, I need to trust Sterling. In order to do that, I need to finish what I started.

He told me his name—but I can't remember it. He told me I needed to be on my guard if I was to ever meet him. He told me he is crafty, cunning, and brilliant. He could make me believe anything if I let him. I don't understand this war. It doesn't make sense that something like this could exist outside of science fiction movies. Maybe that's the reason I shouldn't tell Jane. Maybe it hasn't yet become real enough for me to be able to prepare her.

Note to self- Leader 7, Rank B.

I inhaled slowly, trying to regulate my breathing. It certainly sounded different than the first entry. Whoever Sterling was, I wanted to find him. I had this gnawing guilt eating away at me. Danny died to protect me. Whatever it was he was doing, he was doing for his family. I knew already, so why it took me so long to realize it I cannot be sure. Aidan came to North Bend to kill me. Danny was protecting me—from Aidan.

I told Becky, and just as I expected, she wanted to read more.

"I'm scared," I told her.

"Why?" she asked, raising her voice. "We know now he wasn't a Sevren, don't we?"

I shook my head. "No. We do *not* know that."

"Jane—"

"Please," I said, cutting her off. "Let me prepare myself for the worst before telling myself things because they sound better."

She nodded. "I understand, but we need to keep reading."

July 8th, 2006

Leader 7, Rank B.

"That's it?" she squealed.

"Yeah," I mused. "It…was written at the end of his last entry. Like he was writing something down to remember it. Have no idea what it means."

"Maybe it's some sort of ID?"

I nodded. "Or like a password—code."

She nodded.

"He mentioned war?"

"I was thinking he meant it metaphorically."

"Maybe. It's all too strange. I'm totally confused."

"So am I," she said, almost frantic. "Turn the page!"

July 9th, 2006

. . .

Again Sterling denied my request to bring Jane with me. Sooner or later, she will follow me out one of these nights. Doesn't he realize that would be ten times more dangerous than just letting me tell her everything? She loves me and trusts me. I know she would understand. She would understand that we are simply doing what's right, even if the law doesn't.

He was sounding like a Sevren again. After that entry, it was impossible to put the journal down.

Chapter Six

JULY 10TH, 2006

I've been having these memory dreams lately. Last night, I woke up at around 4 am after an unsettling dream about the first time I met Sterling. It started the night before when I was broken up about the pending divorce that I knew was coming, so I went for a walk. Jane always said that a walk was a good way to clear your head. She was right. I was actually beginning to feel a bit better. That lasted only until a man approached me. He was dressed in a long, hooded cloak like some dark clad figure from a nightmare who should have been accompanied by a giggling side kick. He was very cliché.

"Daniel," he said.

I just stared at him, trying to see his face under his cloak.

"Y-yes?" I stuttered.

"You shouldn't be wondering out in the middle of the night."

I sighed heavily. "Did my dad send you?" I groaned. "Thanks, but really I'm fine."

I pushed past him and kept walking.

"You're in danger," he called.

I turned around. "I promise you," I started, "I'm fine."

He picked up his pace and stopped in front of me again, removing his hood. "Trust me," he said. "You are not fine. You're in danger. I was not sent by anyone. I came on my own account."

"Who are you then?"

"My name is Keller," he said. "Sterling Keller."

"Okay, and how do you know my name?"

"I was a friend of your grandfather's," he said.

I narrowed my eyes. "Who are you...Keller?"

He sighed. "Come with me. We need to talk."

I awoke then. I don't like these dreams. A lot of the memories I had repressed for reasons not completely known to me. It was a very difficult time in my life, and I chose not to remember things. I guess my mind thinks I need to know.

P.S. I think it's pretty stupid to write to a notebook of paper, so all of these entries from now on will actually be addressed. I feel I need to actually write to a real person—someone who will listen.

July 12th, 2006

Dear Jane,

If you are actually reading this, I fear why. It doesn't seem like there would ever be a reason for you to be reading this unless something has happened to me. If something has happened to me, I want you to know that it's all right and that I have made a difference in peoples' lives that you can be proud of me for. If something has happened, it was for the people I love, and it was my choice.

. . .

I had another memory dream last night, and I'm beginning to think that these memory flashes will continue until I remember everything. There must be a reason for surfacing things I have forgotten. I just haven't figured it out yet. Last night, my mind showed me the night I met Sterling just after he had told me who he was. It started the moment he told me why he wanted to speak to me, how he knew my name, and why he had approached me. His hood was down where I could see who he was. His gray hair was hanging in his face messily. It was tangled and stringy. He almost looked homeless, except for the formality of the suit he was wearing. A black, satin-lined jacket and a shirt made out of silk or perhaps suede. The slacks were the traditional black, a perfectly creased addition to the ensemble. It seemed all he was lacking was a top hat. I tried to smile, but I was too confused about what was happening.

"I know I frightened you," he said. "It was not my intent."

I just nodded, sitting on the park bench, trying to ignore the cold. He sat beside me, closer than was comfortable.

"I knew your grandfather very well," he continued. "He was a very smart, very brave man."

"My grandfather was a simple man," I said, "with a simple life. He lived with his wife in a tiny little town in Oregon."

"That tiny little town has a lot of secrets, Daniel."

"Danny."

He nodded. "Danny. That place holds more secrets than you can ever hope to know about. That's why I had to find you."

I didn't know how to respond at first. "You said I was in danger..."

He nodded. "Yes, you are, as is your family."

I instantly felt a sense of anger rising into my chest until it exploded into something more like fury. "Threatening me is one thing," I yelled, standing to my feet, "but you leave my family out of this."

"Threatening?" he bellowed. "Danny, you have it all wrong. I'm warning you. I want to help you. If you want to stay safe and keep those you love safe, then you need me. I, however, also need your help. It was your grandfather's dying wishes that I am fulfilling. Please...just listen."

He went on to tell me that Grandpa was a member of a secret order in the town of North Bend. "I just want to do what your grandfather asked of me," he said.

"Which is what?"

"He asked me to tell you all you need to know when you are old enough to take his place."

My limbs physically started shaking. I was terrified now of what he was going to ask of me.

"Take his place?"

He nodded. "Yes, Danny. It is now your role."

"What is?"

He sighed and dropped his head. "After the death of your grandfather, his order was left leaderless. I took over for the sake of our alliance, but it's time now for you to become the one."

"The one of...what?"

"Leader of an order," he said, "an order that helps people."

"In...in North Bend?"

He nodded.

"How am I to get to North Bend?"

"Let me take care of that," he said. "That simple."

I shook my head. "No. No, I don't want this."

"Danny, listen to me," he demanded, putting his hands on my shoulders. "It is your duty—your fate."

I shrugged him away from me. "I don't believe in fate," I growled. I stormed off, heading for home. He called after me, but I ignored him, only concentrating on staying near my family to make sure nobody could hurt them.

It occurred to me that night that it may just be that taking Grandpa's place was what would keep my family safe. That is what Sterling had said. It also occurred to me that I knew almost nothing about Sterling, and for all I know, he never even knew Grandpa and he was after me for something—or worse, he was after our family.

I stopped for a moment, feeling relief wash over me.

"Are you okay?" Becky asked.

"Yeah," I said. "You were right. Danny would never be a Sevren. How could I ever have even thought he would be? I still can't believe that all of this was going on and I never knew."

"None of us did."

"Yeah, but it's Danny. I should have known."

"You can't do that to yourself, Jane."

I sighed. "I know. It's just hard knowing he was going through this alone."

"I understand."

"We should keep reading."

July 13th, 2006

Dear Jane,

I think I should tell you what happened from the beginning. I think I should explain to you everything that has happened up until now. After that meeting with Sterling, I was constantly terrified. It was almost tortuous, so I had to meet him again. It had been a few days. I went for a walk, knowing he would find me. I didn't even have time to get to the park before he stopped me.

"I'm sorry," I said, "about the way I reacted. You can't expect me to just drop everything and believe you...and more than that—follow you—trust you with my life and the lives of the people I love."

He nodded. "I know," he said, "but I also know the bravery that's in you because I know the bravery that was in your grandfather."

"Then tell me what it is I need to know," I answered. "Tell me these...secrets."

He didn't reply right away, just looked into the darkness like he was searching for the right words to say.

I closed my eyes and inhaled as if for a purpose, as if it would help. But there was no purpose, and it didn't help. I stared into Sterling's eyes and saw layers in them, like layers of lies and secrets. I wished I could mentally push through those layers to the deepest, darkest pages of his subconscious and find out what he was hiding from me. He took a deep breath, and I knew that what he was going to say was something important.

"Bravery isn't being fearless," he started. "Bravery is doing something when you are afraid because it needs to be done."

"Meaning...?"

"Meaning, you can never let fear hold you back. Your grandfather was the bravest man I ever knew," he said, "but he was afraid very much of the time he was with us."

"Who is 'us'?" I asked timidly, almost frightened to speak. "Who exactly are you?"

He gestured to the park bench with his right hand. We took our normal seats.

"We are a group, an alliance if you will, who are vowed to do good for those around us."

I almost smiled. "You're good guys."

He nodded.

"So what is your...alliance?"

He sighed, and again I saw those layers in his eyes. What was he hiding from me?

"Our alliance is one that is against an evil, an evil unknown to most."

He was beginning to sound slightly insane, but the crazier it sounded, the more intrigued I became.

"The evil ones need to be stopped. Simple as that."

"Why not involve the law?" I asked.

"The law?" he bellowed, bringing his face close to mine. "That will not only cause a gruesome war, Danny. It could ruin everything. They are far too clever for the law. They are wide spread—everywhere. That is what we are here for."

"How can you keep something like this a secret?"

"By remembering that this is the only way it can work."

July 16, 2006

. . .

Dear Jane,

It soon became apparent that there was no way of avoiding Sterling. He had been looking for me for far too long, and now it was time for me to help him with what he needed. I was to be appointed with a particular task—one he hadn't yet told me about.

I had to meet him the next night for more information. I had no idea yet if I should trust him. We met at the park as usual. He looked very clean cut compared to the way he did the last couple of times I had seen him. His hair was pulled back in a rubber band and hidden under a hat. He was dressed formally as if coming from a dinner party. I stared into his layered, chestnut eyes, waiting for him to say the first words.

"I am sorry that this all had to come to you," he started. "You are a child as I realize. I believe, Danny, that this is why it will work. Nobody would suspect a child of so much."

"So much what?"

He sighed and looked away from me for a moment. "Our order has a leak."

"Leak." I paused, not fully understanding where Sterling could be going with this.

He nodded. "Many of us have disappeared, only to be found later —murdered."

I think he could see the shock in my eyes, and my mouth hung open.

"I don't mean to frighten you," he said, "but this is why I need you to be brave now, Danny."

I nodded feebly, trying to catch my breath to speak. I couldn't think of anything to say.

"The Silver Wing needs you, Danny. We all need you to help us. I need you to finish what your grandfather started."

I clenched my hands into fists and sucked in a breath of the icy air. "What must I do?"

A small smile spread across Sterling's face. "You must first help me find out who it is that is leaking information. We are losing members rapidly, and nobody can figure out who is against us."

"Wait," I cried out. "Wait. So I am looking for...for a spy?"
He nodded. "Yes," he answered. "A Sevren spy."

July 18th, 2006

Dear Jane,

I have not seen Keller again. I am terrified of what he wants me to do. I fear that I may make a mistake and endanger you and anyone else I care about. I wish I could confide in you, Jane. I wish I could tell you everything—but I can't. I can't say anything if I want to keep you safe. I know Keller has been waiting for me. He says that time is precious and we are running out, but I cannot bring myself to meet him yet. I need time to think and to organize my thoughts before I jump into some crazy mission. I am not sure about any of it anymore. Keller said it is normal to be scared, but what if my fear is what causes me to mess up? What if I ruin everything?

I want you to know that I do intend to tell you everything one way or another. If not in person, then through these words and any others I may write to you. I am just waiting for the right time—waiting until I know how to keep you safe. I do not like keeping secrets from you, but right now that is the only choice I have. I know that this is important, and I do not feel like he has chosen the right person for the job. I am not a hero, Jane. I am just me, and I don't know how to be anyone else.

Chapter Seven

"JANE?" Becky whispered, touching my hand. "Are you okay?"

I looked up from the journal with painfully obvious tension in my features. It was so hard for me to believe everything that Danny had been through.

"All that time," I mused, "and I never knew."

"You couldn't have," she answered. "None of us could have."

I shook my head. "He was my twin. I should have been able to tell."

She touched my hand and sighed. "We've been through this, Jane. You can't do this to yourself. Do you want to take a break for a while?"

I hesitated before responding. "Well, we know now he wasn't a Sevren," I said. "So I think I can be okay not reading anymore today."

"We should go out tomorrow," she said. "Just to get our minds off things. Enjoy our summer as planned."

I tried to smile. "Sounds like a good idea."

I waited for Becky's perkiness to return and waited to hear her chattering about how much fun we would have tomorrow wherever we ended up going, but instead, she ended up falling asleep after an old movie I turned on. I couldn't sleep, so I sat alone on my back porch. The black velvet sky was peppered with sapphire stars. There was a chilly breeze billowing around me, gently ruffling my hair, causing me to draw my blanket closer.

I couldn't help but think about the journal, about Danny, about how he must have felt—a kid back then trusted with a secret so enormous that most of civilization couldn't be told about it. How important that must have made him feel. What did they see in me that made them hesitate? Was it because I was a girl? How different would my life have been if I had been chosen instead of Danny? Would Aidan have been the one to kill me instead? I shivered from that thought, instinctively shying away from it. It was too soon to try to reason out what would have happened if Danny would have still been alive.

It was time for me to call it a night. I had an early day tomorrow with Becky, and I needed to be ready for it. Standing up, I stretched all the kinks out of my back, wondering vaguely how long I had been sitting there as I turned to go in the house.

"Jane."

I whirled around quickly…my hand going up defensively to my throat. A dark figure came out of the brush stealthily. I wanted to run. I was terrified not to, but there was something vaguely familiar about him.

"Who are you?" I asked, my voice not quite steady.

The long, black cloak he had drawn low over his head did a good job of concealing his features from me.

"You know who I am, Jane. I know Danny wouldn't have been able to resist telling you about me."

With a calculated slowness as if he was afraid to frighten me anymore than I already was, he reached up and drew his hood off. I felt the gasp leave my lips. I knew him; I knew that face. I was unsure how, but somehow I recognized the eyes. They were dark and deep, as if a book of a thousand pages could be read within them. They seemed to have…layers. He was a little older than I had imagined. His long, brown hair was still tied back, but there was more silver at the temple, and lines of strain had appeared around his mouth. But those gypsy brown eyes looked exactly the same, had the same power to look into my soul and weigh my worth.

"Sterling."

He nodded his approval at me, beaming like a proud teacher, easing his way up the porch steps. He heaved a sigh and sat down on the swing.

"Please?" he asked quietly. "I'm not as young as I once was, and you are too much like Danny to not ask a lot of questions. There is no reason for us to be uncomfortable as you ask them."

I hesitated only for a second. This was what I wanted, wasn't it? To know everything? To make sense of it all? What could it hurt? Help was just a scream of panic away.

I took that step of faith and eased tentatively on to the far side of the swing, as far from Sterling as I could get, as we stared at each other, both of us trying to determine how to go about it.

"One of your questions, I suspect, is why you are ready now. Well, it's not very easy to explain this, but I couldn't help but notice that you and your pretty friend have been digging around, and I need to warn you that that is not the safest venue."

He gave me a strange look, and I realized that my mouth had dropped open. How on earth could he have known that? However, instead of opening that particular can of worms, I took a different route.

"Will you answer anything that I have to ask? No limits? You will answer it tonight?"

"Yes."

"Okay. Who is leader 7, rank B?"

I could hear his swiftly indrawn breath as he started to reach for me and thought better of it. I had struck a nerve. I didn't know how or even which one, but all the same, that one breath told me volumes, more than all the research Becky and I had tried to do by reading the journal. Danny had been on to something.

"It looks like he told you far more than I thought. No matter. I will start at the beginning."

And he did, telling me about how my grandfather had been in The Silver Wing and how he had approached Danny for help. That is when he got to the missing pieces.

"What very few people understand about the occult is that the myth is always derived from a single grain of truth. They are not just some 'fanciful' lot of people who just have something 'wrong' with them. No. It is almost always something passed down through generations. Sometimes the groups stay small, avoiding detection, allowing the world to go on with their lives. Other times they get noticed. And by people who will stand up, who are willing to make a difference.

"Magnus was one of the original members of The Silver Wing—one of the few men in the village who was courageous enough to step up and try to make a change. It was because of him that we were able to organize into sections and ranks. That we were truly able to make a difference in this war we began to wage. There are nine of our sections with our ranks going up to 'I'. However, there are thirteen sections in The Sevren, and their ranks form all the way up to 'M.'

"Something you need to understand now, Jane, is that everything has a purpose, even down to which road you take to get to work in the morning. It all has a consequence to it. Our fate isn't always tied to our own hands. Sometimes it is held together with our enemy's knots as well. We need to remember that, or all of the world can perish.

"We were getting stronger and arrogant. We thought we could out smart them, so we went against *The Rules*. It—"

"Wait!" I held up my hand interrupting. "What rules?"

"The rules for the fight that has been waging on between the Silver Wing and The Severn for well over a hundred years. Essentially, it is the fight between good and evil. Everything in life needs a balance. There can be no yin without yang, no air without water, no light without darkness…"

"No life without death?" I asked quietly.

"Yes."

"Tell me he didn't die for your game," I demanded harshly, my anger growing with thoughts of my brother. "Tell me Danny wasn't some sacrifice in this madness!"

"Never that child," he said kindly in direct contrast to my anger. "I may have a lot of sins on my soul, but I have never led an innocent lamb to the slaughter. I wish with all of my being that Danny could have been spared."

I could read the sincerity that he had, the strain around his eyes as he thought of my twin and how he couldn't be brought back. I nodded my head for him to continue. Taking a second to collect his thoughts, he started again.

"It has to be fought a certain way—this war. There are rules set down that keep us from going down the wrong path. Whenever one side cheats, the consequences can become dire, so we choose them with care. Both sides have been permitted spies though, which is why it is so difficult to get into The Silver Wing now. Not so much as with the Severn because they will just murder you if you are found out, but since we cannot deal in such ways, it is more difficult for us. We can get lucky though. Sometimes one of them will come to us—they can't take it anymore. They have a sudden kick of conscience or what have you, and they look for us, to join with us and stop The Sevren. But as I said before, there is always a balance. And we can and have lost people too. Sometimes they leave completely, but once in a while, they turn spy. Only one leader was known to be able to do that in all the years we have been in existence, and his name is Magnus.

"A massacre had started the likes of which we had never seen before. It seemed so many of us had begun to mysteriously disappear only to be found in an alleyway, murdered. We knew we had a leak, but we couldn't find out who it was.

"That was Danny's job. Nobody would suspect a mere child of digging around, of being suspicious of what only the leaders could have known about. It was the perfect set up. Our Danny was quite the detective too, never appearing like he knew too much, never asking too many questions and raising alarms. That brilliant young boy found out who it was. Leader 7, Rank B."

"Magnus," I breathed.

"Yes," he said carefully, watching my eyes, gauging my reaction to this news. "Here," he said, reaching into his cloak and pulling out a flask. "This will warm you up, make you feel better, like this was all just a bad dream."

I took a tentative sip of it. It tasted like brandy to me, not my favorite liquor by any means, but I knew it would steady me and give me a little extra warmth when my body had gone so ice cold.

"That is why I have come to you at last, Jane. I need you to finish what Danny started. I need you to prove Magnus's guilt."

"Wait," I said, holding up my hand, trying to understand what he was saying. My eyes were getting heavy, and my brain was starting to feel sluggish as I tried to comprehend what Sterling just told me. "You mean this guy is still on your team after what happened to Danny?"

"I told you, Jane," he said sadly. "There are rules that have to be followed. And this is one of them. No proof could be brought to me before Danny was murdered, so the accusation had to die with him. Then the murders stopped suddenly, and some believed that the person behind them had proved too risky and had been taken care of. But I didn't believe it—I couldn't. It was too good to be true."

I tried to pay attention, but the porch had begun to spin, and my head was getting so heavy I could barely lift it. I looked at Sterling for answers with panic in my eyes.

"It's okay, Jane. It's just a sleeping herb laced in the brandy to help you sleep deeply tonight. I don't want you to get any nightmares."

Carefully, he picked me up and carried me to the back door. Opening it soundlessly, he carried me up to my room and laid me carefully on my cool sheets, tugging up my comforter to keep me warm.

I wanted to say something, but I couldn't. I could feel sleep coming like an avenging angel ready to carry me away. But I needed to know why they needed me now. What had changed? As if he could read my thoughts, Sterling gently took my hand and answered my unasked question. And as I fell into a deep, black oblivion, I heard the urgency in his voice as he told me.

"He's back, Jane. The murders have started again."

Chapter Eight

I AWOKE WITH A THROBBING HEADACHE. I sat up, groaning, still feeling like I hadn't slept. Becky was still asleep, so I took my time with a hot shower to try and clear my head to figure out what happened.

"God, I'm an idiot," I murmured out loud. I knew something was off about Sterling, and I still took a drink from him. I shouldn't have been surprised he drugged me. I knew I had to tell Becky, but I wasn't sure how. I just stood under the water, going over and over it in my head. A knock scattered my thoughts.

"Jane?" Becky called from outside the door. "You okay?"

"Uh...yeah. I'll be out in a minute."

"No rush. I'm just making sure."

I immediately turned the water off and wrapped myself in a towel.

"Becky, I need to talk to you."

"Are you okay?"

"Something happened last night."

I told her everything about the night before, from meeting Sterling to the throbbing in my head.

For a moment, Becky just stared at me as if all the words ever created weren't enough to convey what she was feeling. I couldn't say any more either. The silence was maddening, not knowing what she was thinking or what she would say. I had to be the first to break it.

"What do I do?"

Her eyes became even tenser when she opened her mouth to speak. At first, all she did was mutter something nonsensical. "Uh...I...I don't know. Maybe there isn't anything we can do."

"There has to be something." My voice was almost a whisper like I was frightened to speak it out loud. I didn't want it to be real.

"Well, then we need help," she said. "You know that as well as me."

I nodded.

"And something else I have to say," she started sternly. "We are in this together. No buts and no conditions. Together, okay?"

"Promise."

"Now, we need some help."

"How do you propose we get help?" I asked. "Really, Becky. This isn't just some scavenger hunt. This is dangerous. This is something that even I can't comprehend the risks of."

She nodded, breaking eye contact.

"What are you thinking?" I asked.

"I think I have an idea," she said, "but...you won't like it."

I just stared at her, waiting for her to come clean. "God, Becky, just tell me before I have a nervous breakdown."

I actually thought I saw her smile before she replied. "We need...we need *him*."

I was about to ask her who when my mind halted, and a screeching sound rang in my ears. My voice swelled into my throat, and I almost yelled at her. "What? No way, Becky."

"Jane, think about it. There's nothing else we can do. He is the only one who can help us. He is the *only* one with the skills and knowledge we need."

My eyes began burning as I fought that familiar feeling. "Why can't I ever escape him?" I yelled. "Why does everything that happens to me have to involve him? How do we know he's not behind this?"

"We don't," she said, "but what does your heart tell you? Please,

Jane. You know now that everything he did he did out of love. You know that now."

My face burned, and I shook my head. "That isn't fair."

She bowed her head then looked away from me. "I'm sorry," she whispered. "Please trust me. This one time."

"I don't know. What if he knows nothing? Then if we tell him, he will get himself involved even if we change our minds."

"Then let's talk to him," she said. "Let's see what he knows."

"And if he knows nothing?"

"Then I am as lost as you are for ideas."

I mimicked her sigh and just focused on trying to regulate my breathing to stay composed. I had no idea how this was going to play out.

I didn't bother calling him, only because I knew where he would be. I left with Becky to the coffee shop, and sure enough, he was at his usual table with some book on the scientific method, unaware I was there.

"Aidan?"

He turned around, instantly smiling. I tried to ignore how adorable he was.

"So now you want to talk?" he teased, still smiling.

"Sort of," I said, nodding. "I just need to know something."

He closed the book he was reading and gestured for me to sit. "Okay," he said. "What is it?"

Becky and I sat down, and at first, I couldn't say anything.

"Jane," I heard Becky murmur, "just ask him."

"Ask me what?"

I suddenly couldn't look at him. Everything flooded back to me, and I found myself feeling sick again. What was I thinking?

"Never mind," I said, getting up from the table. "Never mind. It's nothing."

"I know you better than that," he said before I had time to turn away. "So what's going on?"

"Is it so hard to believe that I just don't want anything to do with you?"

"Why are you here, Jane?" He raised his eyebrows at me.

I clenched my hands into fists. This was more about Aidan than I wanted to admit. I could almost feel the tension. I glanced at Becky, and she nodded regretfully.

"Damn." I sat down beside him and leaned closer than was comfortable to keep quiet.

"Who the hell is Sterling Keller?"

His eyes immediately went dark, and his mouth hung open. "Where did you hear that name?"

"No!" I retorted. "Do *not* answer my question with a question, Aidan. Who is he?"

"Jane, I can't answer that question," he said, tension rising in his voice. "Not until you tell me what's going on."

"God!" I grunted. "Why is it so impossible to *not* involve you in everything?"

"Because our lives have affected each other's in unavoidable ways, and because of that, they will always be bringing us back to one another. You know that!"

I put my head in my hands.

"Just tell him," Becky said.

"Great," Aidan announced, throwing his hands up. "She knows too?"

"Oh, please," I grunted with an unnecessary amount of sarcasm. "Like she wouldn't find out anyway. This is Becky we're talking about— the girl who hid unseen on the floor of your car. Besides, you know I'm a terrible liar."

"That's not the point," he said. "Tell me what you know."

I shook my head. "You first."

"Jane—"

"*You* first!"

He huffed. "I…can't."

"Fine," I said, getting up from the table. "If you won't talk to me, I guess I don't need your help after all."

"Help?" he yelled.

Damn. Did I say help?

"Jane, sit down," he demanded. "What's going on?"

I didn't want to tell him in case he didn't know anything that could help us. I didn't want him involved unless there was no way around it.

"His…name…his name is in Danny's journal," I said, "and I just want to know who he is."

I figured that was acceptable, considering it was the truth—just not all of it.

He sighed. "Sterling Keller is a member of The Silver Wing," he said. "One of the leaders."

"Does he know Walter?"

He shook his head. "The leaders don't usually know each other."

I narrowed my eyes. "Then how do you?"

He chuckled. "Jane, you forget who I am. When it comes to the Sevren and The Silver Wing, I make it a point to know more than most. We stay safe and hidden that way."

"So what you're telling me is that Danny was a member of The Silver Wing?"

He nodded.

"How long have you known?"

He put his hands up defensively. "I swear I didn't!" he said. "I mean…I had a hunch, sure, but until you mentioned Keller's name, I didn't know!"

"Well, next time you decide to have a 'hunch,' Aidan, tell me!"

He nodded. "I will. Is there anything else?"

I shook my head. "Is that all you know?"

He nodded. "Yes. That's all."

I turned away when I heard him say something else.

"But that's not all *you* know, is it?"

"What?" I snapped, trying to sound surprised and honest. "What is *that* supposed to mean?"

"Jane, you suck at lying, so give it up."

I inhaled slowly, trying to keep up the act. It took me less than ten seconds to realize it was useless and that Aidan knew me better than I wanted to admit. I huffed and sat back down.

"No," I admitted, almost shamefully. "It's not."

"Then tell me what you know," he said. "And don't lie to me."

He would know right away if I was lying, but I couldn't tell him everything. If I mentioned that I met Sterling, then there would be no way of avoiding him getting completely submerged in my life again. I tried to think of how to start. His uneven breathing told me he wasn't being patient, and it made me ten times more nervous. He stared at me as if trying to read my mind. I felt like I had to say something—anything to get him to stop looking at me that way.

"Okay," I started. "I knew Danny was a member of The Silver Wing. He talked about it in his journal. He also mentioned that he was supposed to take me with him someday. I feel it is my job to finish what he started and my responsibility to find out who is Leader 7, Rank B."

Aidan froze. His mouth was agape, and he appeared as hard as stone. He held so still that it actually startled me when he finally moved.

"What?" he choked out. "That last part, Jane? Can you repeat that?"

His reaction terrified me, and I almost lost the courage to speak. What did I say wrong? "L-leader 7…"

"Rank B?"

I nodded. "Yes," I whispered.

He put his hand over his mouth and dropped his head. "Shit," he murmured.

I could literally feel my heart pounding like it would tear through my chest. I immediately regretted telling him anything. He sighed and lifted his head, running his hands through his hair.

"What?" It was all I could say.

He just locked eyes with me without saying a word. He stared until I averted my gaze back down at the table.

"We need to go!" he demanded, instantly standing up from the table. "Now."

"What?"

He gently grasped my hand. "Come on," he said.

"Both of you."

Becky nodded and stood up, eyeing me. I followed Aidan out to the parking lot. He was practically running to the car.

"Get in," he demanded.

I shook my head. "I'll follow you."

"Jane—get in. I'll bring you back to get your car later. Now!"

I raised my hands. "Fine," I murmured.

I got in the passenger's seat, and Becky crawled into the back, still not saying a word. Silence from Becky could only mean one of two things. She was either terrified or furious. I was almost afraid to know which. I looked back at her, and she mouthed, "I'm sorry."

I just nodded, unable to say anything. Aidan got in and started the engine, speeding out of the parking lot before I had time to grab the door for support. I heard Becky gasp, but she didn't even snap at him to slow down, and I wouldn't dare. The drive was silent until he pulled over into the parking lot of a hotel.

I observed the building, my eyes scanning the two-story complex. "Is this where you're staying?"

He nodded. "This is where 'Josh Coville' is staying." He winked at me, and I thought I saw a glimpse of a smile.

I shook my head. *Of course.*

We followed him to the second floor to room "213." As soon as I walked in, I felt that dreamy sensation of the past. I recognized the room almost like home. I had spent about a week in the same kind of room when Ian came to save me. It seemed like a lifetime ago.

Aidan sighed and sat on the edge of the double bed, signaling at us to join him. I pulled a wooden chair away from the little round table and sat in front of him, not wanting to be too close. Becky mimicked me completely as if she didn't know what to do.

"What's going on?" I asked. "This is what I wanted to avoid."

He nodded. "I know. But when you said those words, Jane—Leader 7, Rank B—it's not something I can just ignore."

"I am guessing then that you know who he is?"

He shook his head. "I know more than anyone else does."

I narrowed my eyes. "Meaning what exactly?"

He sighed again, running his hand through his hair. "Jane, do you remember the license plate of Abraham's car?"

I shook my head. "Not really," I answered. "I remember it spelled 'Sevren' with missing letters."

He nodded. "Yes." He reached behind him, digging a notebook out of his school bag and jotting something down. He handed it to me.

"Look familiar?"

I stared at the letters.

SEVRNB7

I hesitantly handed the notebook to Becky, and her mouth fell open.

"So…Abraham?" I said. "Leader 7 was Abraham?"

"No," Aidan said, shaking his head. "The car wasn't actually his."

"He stole the car?"

Aidan bitterly chuckled. "Does that really surprise you?"

"I…guess it shouldn't."

"Look," he started. "I understand better than you think I do."

"Really." It wasn't a question, but he answered it anyway.

"Yes," he said. "I do. I *know* you don't want me involved in this."

"I feel a 'but' coming."

He smiled. "But…you *do* need my help whether you want to admit it or not."

I just stared at his face for a moment. The near perfection of his beauty didn't seem so magical anymore. He was just Aidan Summers. The man I loved and hated at the same time. I tore my gaze away from him and back to Becky. It was killing me to see the look on her face. Her eyebrows were pulled together, and her lips were slightly trembling as if it was taking every ounce of strength she had to not break down in tears.

"Please say something," I whispered to her. "Please."

"What do you want me to say?"

I didn't answer. I just needed to hear her voice. Her silence was worse than anything she could say.

"So," Aidan continued, bringing my eyes back to his, "is there anything else, Jane?"

My heartbeat sped up, and heat rushed to my cheeks. "No."

He sighed and fell backward on the bed. "You sure?" he asked.

"Yes."

He instantly sat back up and stared at me with raised eyebrows. "Okay," he said. "Then what was it you were saying about finishing what Danny started?"

I almost felt my breath explode when I realized he actually believed me. "I am supposed to find something," I said.

"In order to do that, Jane, you need to know what he was doing."

I couldn't tell him I met Sterling, so I said the only other thing I could. "Do you know?" I asked.

He dropped his head. "I might," he answered, "but I have a few questions that I need answered to be sure."

I nodded. "Okay."

"How are you getting these…answers?" Becky asked. Her voice was still only a whisper.

"I need to see some people," he said. "More detail than that is not necessary."

I sighed. Of course he would say something like that. We had to tell him everything *we* knew, but it was okay for him to keep secrets.

"Come on. I'll take you back to get your car."

We followed him out the door without saying a word. The drive was silent, but I knew he wanted to say something. I ignored the uncomfortable feeling and unbuckled my seat belt before he even stopped the car.

I got out, and he called after me.

"Jane?"

I turned around, trying to avoid eye contact.

"Can you meet me here tomorrow?"

"Why?"

"Can you meet me or not?"

"Fine," I said. "Tomorrow."

"Oh, and Jane?"

I turned around, again trying to avoid his eyes.

"Just…stay at home until then please. Be…be safe."

Chapter Nine

I WAS HOPING we could wait until we got home to talk, but Becky couldn't keep a single thought to herself.

"We need to finish the journal," she said as we pulled away from the café.

"I know," I answered soberly, keeping my eyes on the road.

"I think we will need to do this ourselves, Jane."

"I agree. I don't trust Aidan knows as much as he thinks."

She nodded. "It seems like he wants to help us, but you know as well as I do that he tends to do things the hard way."

"That's because if it's dangerous, he feels there must be another way."

"Yes—and sometimes there isn't."

We drove on toward my house, the setting sun behind us, brilliant in my rear-view mirror. Too many emotions pulled at my chest—uncertainty, fear, anxiety of how all this was going to play out.

I shook my head, my tense grip increasing on the steering wheel. "I can't deal with this alone, Becky. I feel like I need to be back home—with you."

She nodded. "I know, and you shouldn't have to do this alone. We're in this together."

"What will my mom say?" I groaned, remembering the first time I left her and how hard she took it.

"She knew you were going to go back eventually, didn't she?"

"Yeah, but we haven't talked about it yet. I'm kind of springing it on her out of the blue."

She shrugged. "Just talk to her. I'm sure she'll understand."

I exhaled sharply. "Will you tell her with me?"

She gave me a synthetic smile. "I think this is one you should do alone."

"Yeah, I guess you're right. I just have to find the right way to tell her. I don't want to hurt her, and I hate lying, but I obviously can't be completely honest about everything." I sighed.

"I'm sure you'll think of something. Just don't let it slip out and spill the beans."

I chuckled. "I'll try not to."

My tight grip loosened, and a sadness came over me at the thought of leaving my mom again. But Becky and I had to figure all this out. We owed it to Danny. I wouldn't let him down, not this time. "When I get back home to North Bend, we can get started on some research."

"Okay. Good idea," she said. "And Aidan? He's not going to let this go no matter how much you tell him you don't want him involved."

I scoffed and rolled my eyes despite the slight smile breaking its way to my lips at the thought of him still being so protective of me. "I know. I actually have an idea though."

I knew what the next step was, and now that I was going back home, I had to take that step despite the fear and uncertainty. I was shaking before I even picked up the phone.

"Jane, relax," Becky said. "It's going to be fine."

I exhaled slowly and dialed the number on the business card in my hand. I put the phone on speaker and heard a distantly familiar voice answer.

"Detective Styles."

"Yes, this is Jane Callahan. I'm not sure if you remember me—"

"I do," he interrupted. "Daniel's sister. Do you have any new information?"

"I'm not sure. I was hoping we could talk about it."

"Can you come into the office?"

"I'm actually not in California. I'll be back in North Bend, Oregon soon though."

"North Bend, huh?" He paused. "I actually know someone in that town. Great man. Great detective. I'll tell you what. I'll contact him and send him the case files. It might be helpful to meet with someone face to face, and the more people on this case the better."

I glanced at Becky, and she nodded.

"Sure," I said. "Thank you."

"Ask for Detective Wolmack."

"Thank you, Detective Styles. I really appreciate it."

"Of course. I'll stay in contact with him as well. And I'm always just a phone call away if you need to discuss anything further." He paused. "I...I'm not really supposed to say anything, but Daniel's case is one that still keeps me up at night. The case may be closed, but that doesn't mean I have stopped trying to figure out what I missed. I want you and your parents to know that."

"That means a lot to me. Thank you."

"I look forward to hearing about your meeting. Good luck to you."

"Thanks. Bye."

I hung up the phone and exhaled deeply.

"Are you okay?" Becky asked.

"I will be."

"Where were you?" he demanded.

"Sorry," I answered. "I forgot."

"You forgot?"

"Yes."

"How can you forget?"

I sensed Becky shift uncomfortably at my side. "I've had a lot on my mind, Aidan, okay?"

"A lot on your mind?"

"Yes. I've decided to go back to North Bend. I haven't figured out how to tell my mom yet. Is that enough for you?"

"Geez, sorry," he grumbled. "I'm glad you're going back though. It's not the same there without you."

"Yeah, whatever. So I'm here. What did you want to talk about? Did you find out what Danny was doing?"

He shook his head. "Not entirely," he said. "But I *did* find out some details."

"Like what?"

"Like how they had a leak in their alliance, and it was Danny's job to pin the guilt on a man named Magnus."

I already knew that, so I didn't reply.

"It was his job to dig up dirt and prove it was Magnus who was the one responsible for deaths and disappearances in The Silver Wing."

He stopped and narrowed his eyes at me.

"What?" I asked bitterly.

"Jane—is there any reason you aren't shooting off a wave of questions like a machine gun?"

"What are you talking about?"

"I usually can't get through more than one sentence without you interrupting to ask who or what or why or—*something*."

"I was listening."

"Listening?"

"Yes."

He sighed. "Don't make me ask you."

"Ask me what?"

He huffed, and an angry expression danced across his features until he regained control. "Ask you what it is you aren't telling me."

So much for not being able to read me.

"Tell me now, or I am not saying another word."

I heard Becky sigh. "Just tell him," she whispered.

"Fine," I replied almost venomously. "I found all of that out already."

"From who?" he asked. "Or what?"

"It was a who," I answered.

He looked like he was becoming frantic. I could hardly bear to say the name out loud. I was terrified of what he would say and how angry we would be. My voice was only a whisper.

"Keller."

"Keller?" he spat, trying to stay quiet. He stood to his feet, pointing at me. "Sterling Keller?"

"Aidan, calm down!" I hissed. "This place is not exactly private."

He sat back down and squeezed the bridge of his nose. "Why didn't you tell me you met Sterling?"

"Because I didn't want you involved any more than you had to be."

"Jane, you can't just tell me some things and leave out pieces. There is no way I can help you unless I know everything."

"Then I have a condition."

"Are you serious?" he demanded. "You're going to make ultimatums now?"

"Yes. If I have to tell you everything, I want you to tell me everything. If I can't keep secrets, neither can you."

He grumbled. "The only reason I keep things from you is—"

"To keep me safe because you love me—yada, yada, yada."

He chuckled. "Actually, I was going to say because it's easier to deal with things if you don't know about them."

I huffed. "Whatever."

I knew I had to tell my mom about my plans, but I couldn't stop thinking about the shattered look on her face when I first left California. I dreaded putting her through that again. I took a deep breath, trying to muster my courage, and walked into the kitchen.

"Mom?"

She turned away from the stove for a moment, wooden spoon in hand. "Hi, sweetie. Making chili. Sound okay?"

"Yeah, great but...um..."

"What is it?" She turned away from the stove again and looked into my eyes. I immediately felt my courage evaporating.

"Um...I was thinking maybe..."

"Jane, please just spit it out." She smiled when she said it, but I could tell she was annoyed.

"I was thinking about going back home—I mean...not home but..."

"You want to go back to your dad's?"

I nodded. "North Bend. With Becky."

She set the spoon on a plate, turned off the burner, and took a seat at the kitchen table. I sat across from her, afraid to look her in the eyes. When I finally made eye contact, she didn't look anything like I feared. I didn't see the expression of pain I did the first time I left.

"What brought this on?" she asked.

I knew I couldn't tell her the truth, so I settled for something reasonable. "It's not that I don't love living with you because of course I do. It's just...all of my friends are in North Bend, and I want to finish high school there. I don't want to go to another new school when I have only one year left."

She nodded. "Okay. If it's what you want. Are you sure you're okay though? You seem like something's wrong."

"No," I said, clearing my throat. "I was just afraid of what you were going to say."

She smiled. "It's okay, honey. I was expecting it at some point. I'm actually surprised it took you this long to spill it."

The twisting in my stomach lessened as I took in that sparkle in her eye that always made me smile.

"You know me better than I am comfortable with."

She chuckled. "Get used to it, kiddo."

After realizing I was finally going back to North Bend, I found myself anxious to get there. I already missed Becky, and she had just left three days ago. After all the excitement, the day still snuck up on me, and I ended up rushing through the last hour of packing. Once again, I found myself in a completely empty bedroom, prepared to leave my mother. She seemed to be handling it much better than before and didn't even cry at the airport.

"Are you sure you want to stay here, Mom?"

She smiled and pulled me into a hug. "I'm sure."

"Do you think you'll ever go back to California?"

"Maybe someday. I like it here though. It's home, at least for now."

"I'll come visit soon. I promise."

I pulled away and looked into her eyes. She really seemed fine with the situation, but I still couldn't help feeling like I was abandoning her. I knew as I did before that this was the right decision for me.

With one last hug and unexpected tears forming in my eyes, I boarded the plane that would take me home.

It was déjà vu when Ethan pulled me into that almost rib-cracking, bear hug, but the smile I gave him wasn't the same at all. Rather than nervous and uncertain, I was excited and happy to be back. Even the cold and the rain were welcoming. As soon as I got home, I threw my bags on my bed, stuffed a couple bucks in my pocket, and headed down to Books by the Bay to see Becky. She greeted me with a huge grin and a hug like she hadn't seen me in years.

"Hey," I said.

"Good to be back?"

"Definitely!"

"I don't want to spoil your first day back, but we need to get started on that research you mentioned. Summer is almost over, and we won't have time during school."

I nodded. "I agree."

"How's Friday?"

I smiled, remembering our old sleepovers. "Sounds good."

I knew Ethan wanted to talk to me, so I sat down at the kitchen table.

"Hey," he said, cheerful as ever. "Glad to be back?"

"I am. It just feels like home here."

He smiled. "It makes me happy to hear you say that. I was thinking we could go out to eat tonight. Maybe catch up some."

There was so much I couldn't tell my dad, so much I was afraid of spilling if I said too much. The look in his eyes was impossible to refuse though.

"Sure," I said. "I'm supposed to meet Becky, but it can wait."

Ethan's face lit up. I realized how much I missed him when he looked at me like that.

A knock came at the door, and Ethan perked up.

"I got it," I said. I opened the door, fully expecting to see Becky.

"Rudy!" I immediately hugged him, realizing it felt like no time at all had passed. Rudy was always so familiar and made me feel normal in the best way.

He wrapped his strong arms around my waist. "It's so good to see you, Jane. It's been way too long. I've missed you," Rudy said, increasing the pressure of his embrace and lifting me gently.

"Hey, Rudy," I heard Ethan say as he walked over to the door.

Rudy released his hold on me and nodded to my dad. "Hi, Mr. Callahan."

"I was just taking Jane out for a bite. Would you like to join us?"

A huge smile spread across Rudy's face. "I'd love to. Thanks."

We headed down to one of the limited number of restaurants in North Bend. I smiled remembering how small and still things seemed here. I loved the slowness and the quiet. There were almost no cars, and very few people even owned cell phones. It was different here, but I never felt more at home.

Rudy and Ethan chattered about random topics, but I wasn't listening until I heard my name.

"You awake over there?" Rudy asked, still with that heartwarming smile on his face.

"Yeah. Sorry," I said. "I was thinking."

"About what?"

"Just how glad I am to be back."

By the time Friday night came along, Becky and I decided there was no reason we had to tell Aidan anything if he wasn't going to tell us anything. I knew the first thing we had to do was talk to Detective Wolmack.

We sauntered in, already nervous, and approached the main desk at the front.

"Can I help you?" an older woman asked with a cheery smile on her face.

"Hi…um…we're looking for Detective Wolmack."

"Wolmack. Sure." She picked up her phone and dialed three numbers. "Detective, there are two young ladies here to see you. Okay. I'll send them in. Thank you." She hung up the phone. "You can head on in. His office is in the far-right corner in the back."

I nodded. "Thank you."

We pushed through the door, revealing the main office area. People were bustling around, and phones were ringing, but it wasn't quite as crowded and noisy as it is in the movies.

We headed toward the back, weaving around the desks. A middle-aged man emerged from the corner office in the back and took a sip from his mug while scanning the room.

I approached him, not sure what to say.

"Can I help you?" he asked, irritation behind his words.

I couldn't speak at first. I took a deep breath and forced the words from my mouth. "Detective Wolmack?"

"Yes."

"My name is Jane Callahan," I said. "Detective Styles sent me. He said I could talk to you."

He closed his eyes and nodded. "Yes, I remember."

"We understand that you cannot discuss an ongoing case, but what about one that is already closed?"

He signaled us with his hand to follow him and led us into his office.

"Take a seat," he said, gesturing to the leather chairs in front of his desk.

I looked down at my hands, picking at my nail polish. "Thank you." I met his gaze. "Have you found out anything else that we don't know?"

He shook his head. "No. But Detective Styles noted in the case file that a young man stopped by a while ago and said he had information."

"Aidan." I said it before I could stop myself.

Wolmack pulled his eyebrows together. "No." He shook his head slightly. "According to the note, it was someone by the name of"—he quickly flipped through the pages on his desk, squinting at the paper held close to his face—"Josh."

I almost had to hold my breath to keep from laughing.

"What did he say?" Becky chimed in.

"I'm afraid I can't tell you that," he said, "but it doesn't seem to have been very helpful."

I sighed.

"I know you want to know what happened to your brother, but there just isn't enough."

"But what if we can find more?" Becky asked. "What if we find something—something useful? Would you re-open the case?"

He nodded. "Possibly, though I doubt you will be able to find anything."

"We can try."

"There is one thing," he started. He licked his thumb and leafed through the paperwork, zeroing in on a specific page. He snatched his reading glasses from the breast pocket of his white shirt and slid them on. "It looks like there were a few people that mentioned they saw a tall, thin man with long hair in a baseball cap at the scene around the time the bod —*he* was found. He was reported being seen at other significant times and places as well. That's all I can tell you."

I nodded. Magnus. I knew it had to be him.

"Thank you," I said.

"I'm sorry we haven't been able to do more for your brother," he said. I could feel the sorrow in his voice. "But I know Styles, and I know he won't give up."

I nodded in return. "I know. Thank you for your time."

He stood and offered his hand. "Thank you for coming in, Miss Callahan."

I shook his hand lightly as his sympathetic eyes held mine. I wrenched open the large, wooden door, and Becky and I weaved through the desks in the main office, heading for the front door.

When we got back to the car, the tension was so thick I had to say something just to break the silence.

"I don't want Aidan involved," I said.

Becky nodded. "Neither do I," she answered dryly. She turned toward me. "We need to find some things out for ourselves."

We went to her place where we would have more privacy. We decided to study in the den even though it was a little shabby. It consisted of a ratty couch, an entertainment center, and sheer white curtains. It wasn't necessarily the most comfortable room in the house, but once we finished throwing all the blankets and pillows on the floor, it started to feel more like home. I put in one of those B-rated scary movies that had terrible graphics but could still manage to make you jump. As I rapidly threw together the dip for our chips, I laughed as Becky walked around, turning on all the lights to "brighten up the place." She was always a chicken when it came to scary movies.

I found a comfortable place on the couch, and Becky plopped down on the floor. I had a book from the reference library while she stared intently at the screen of her laptop. Curious, I peered over to see what she was reading.

I laughed quietly. "I don't think looking up scripts on ancient cults is going to help much."

"It *has* to involve The Sevren," she said stubbornly, still refusing to avert her gaze.

"Kind of focused there, aren't you?" I threw a potato chip at her.

"Knock it off," she said, throwing it back at me and adding two of her own. "This is serious work."

She glanced up at the TV and screamed when she saw the generic axe murderer hacking into the pretty young girl.

"Oh my God!" I yelled in a fake, horrified voice. "She looks like you, Becky! You're next. He's after you."

"That's not funny!" she shrieked out. "What if he really is?"

"Oh, he totally is."

"Seriously, we need to focus."

"You're the one who's scared."

"Well, you aren't helping," she whined. "You know me. Even when I'm at home alone and I hear a noise I get scared."

I chuckled. "Even when you're home not alone you get scared."

"Hey," she breathed. "I'm not that bad."

I just shook my head, trying to suppress the urge to laugh at her.

"We really do need to focus here, Jane," she said. "It would be best to turn the movie off."

That time I did laugh. "Nice try."

She huffed. "Fine, but if you can't stay focused, then I am turning it off anyway."

She had a tone behind her words that made it seem like I had actually hurt her feelings somehow.

"Hey, you know I'm just kidding with you, right?"

She turned around and smiled at me. "Yeah, yeah."

"No, really. I get scared too you know."

"Just not as easily as me?"

"Right."

"Fine. Are you scared now?"

I laughed. "Over a cheesy movie? Not a chance."

"Well, maybe being scared of a movie is a little silly, but after all the craziness you went through, it isn't illogical to be easily spooked," she said. "I mean...I'm afraid of real things."

"Like what?"

"Like when you are afraid to cross a dark room simply because you have no idea what might be lurking."

I nodded. "Or like when you were a kid and afraid to look out the window because someone might be looking back."

She nodded. "Exactly."

"It would be scary even now."

We looked over simultaneously as the curtains rustled with the breeze, adding to Becky's discomfort.

"Wouldn't that be creepy?"

I suddenly felt that odd sense of being watched. Even sure that it was paranoia, it had me concerned. It was deep in my gut, almost a tingle, like when you know someone is staring at you even without turning around. I saw Becky shudder, and we both glanced one more time as the curtains moved again. She shook her head, quietly laughing at how impractical we were being.

She locked her gaze back at her laptop.

That tingle wasn't diminishing. I was beginning to understand what Aidan meant when he said he sensed danger. I felt as if I was experiencing the same thing. I looked over again at the window, and, of course, being the person I am, the wind blew the curtain just far enough to reveal a pair of almost burning eyes staring at me. Panic shot through me as I took notice of the pasty, white face with greasy black hair and yellowed teeth revealed by a vile grin.

I tried to scream but was nearly paralyzed. I gripped Becky's shoulder, digging in my fingernails.

"Ow!" she whined. "Stop trying to scare—"

Her sentence was cut short by an ear-shattering wail. Her scream snapped us to action, and I grabbed the knife I used to chop up the chives for our dip, and we tore down the hallway, slamming into walls as we struggled to get to the bathroom before he got to us. We knew he was after us.

Finally getting to the bathroom, I slammed the door shut. With my heart racing and hands shaking, I struggled to lock the door.

"Hurry!" Becky yelled, getting hysterical. "Hurry! For the love of God, lock the door!"

The lock finally snapped into place. Becky was now hyperventilating, and she pulled out her cell phone. Her hands were shaking so badly she kept dropping it.

I took the phone from her and signaled for her to sit on the edge of the bathtub to catch her breath and dialed Aidan's number. If it was ever possible for someone to get used to their life being in danger, I guess I had to be getting pretty good at it by this point.

"Jane? What's wrong?"

He always knew when something had happened. "You need to get here," I said. "There was someone here...outside the window. He was watching us!"

"Was it Keller?"

"What?" I mused. "No. I would have said 'Keller.' This guy was someone else."

"Okay. I'm on my way. I won't be long."

My heart was pounding the entire time we waited for him, but I had to stay strong for Becky's sake. It wasn't fair that she had to be pulled into my problems.

"Where is he?" she said, weeping. "Is he coming? Does he know where I live. Is—?"

"Becky," I interrupted, touching her shoulder. "He's on his way. Everything's going to be fine."

She breathed out an almost silent "okay."

I sighed, running my hands through my hair.

"We screwed up, didn't we?"

I brought my gaze back to hers. "Uh…yeah," I answered reluctantly. "Big time."

"Great."

Becky's phone vibrated, and she shrieked, jumping almost five inches from the edge of the tub.

"It's just Aidan," I said. "He's here."

It seemed like it took forever for Aidan to get there, when in reality it hadn't taken him longer than five minutes because he so conveniently happened to be "in the neighborhood."

Instead of waiting for his knock, we knew he would protect us and slowly stepped out of the bathroom, checking to make sure we were alone, then raced to the front door to meet him. Seeing Becky's terrified face, he assured her we were safe.

"It's okay," he said. "He's gone now."

She nodded. "Gone where?" she asked.

"Just gone," he said. "I'm telling you we're safe."

"Right," she replied, still shaking. "I knew that."

She wouldn't make eye contact with either of us.

Aidan gazed at her with a lost look on his face, ready to say something until he looked to me, and I shook my head. Becky needed to come to terms with this her own way. It would be best for him to not say anything. He nodded in understanding and grabbed my hand, leading me outside to the window. Becky trailed behind. He crouched low to the ground and pointed out the footprints.

"He must have been pacing," he said, "to get a better view of you."

A chill spread through my body as my hands drifted up to clutch my arms, and I felt Becky shudder beside me. I squinted my eyes, observing the footprints. While I was outdoorsy, I had never been a girl scout, so I had to take his word for it. Standing up, he brushed off his pants.

"Come on," he said. "Let's go back inside. I'll stay with you for a while until you feel better."

When we got back to the den, Becky immediately turned off the TV while another gruesome horror scene was playing. She strode over to the pile of blankets and pillows on the floor. She flopped down and pulled a pillow into her lap. She looked me square in the face.

"Jane," she started, "I love you, but I am *never* watching another scary movie with you as long as I live!"

We decided it was a good idea to relax for the next couple of days to straighten out our thoughts and try to trust Aidan in keeping us safe. Relaxing was impossible for me. The only thing I could think about was what we were missing. I opened Danny's journal to read the last entries. I had been putting it off because the idea of his journal ending made me feel like he was slipping away—like I was losing him all over again. I couldn't put it off any longer.

July 26th, 2006

Dear Jane,

It's become clear that this task is more dangerous than I realized. It's also become clear that you are not someone I want involved. This is not the only thing I have written to you. This is only part of something very important that I need to tell you. In case this journal was to fall into the wrong hands, I cannot tell you everything here. Just remember the good times and the fun we used to have at the river over the summer,

Jane. Remember me, and you will find everything you need to. I love you.

I sighed. How was the river supposed to help me find what he was talking about? I turned the page.

July 27th, 2006

Jane,

Remember the river from our summers? Do you remember the tree that always grew into a heart shape? Do you remember that tin I called my treasure box?

That was it. Three questions. The river, the tree, the tin. A curious suspicion was rising. There was something about Sterling and The Silver Wing that was eating at me. There was a missing piece. Ethan had mentioned wanting to have an early dinner with me tonight before his shift at the hospital, but I needed some time to clear my head. I felt terrible for running off again, but I felt I had no other choice. I would be useless for conversation with so much on my mind.

I drove down toward Nasika Park past North Bend. The drive itself was helpful for escaping. The road was narrow and empty. Trees of the brightest green loomed over the street, coming together in a canopy of solitude. Farther down, the leaves became darker shades of green and dappled the sunlight in spots along the road. I stopped the car at the top of the hill to make it down to the creek on foot. A figure came into view. Blue jeans and a familiar, low-cut, red sweater. A small gasp escaped. It could only be Becky, but why was she here? And…why was she crying? I didn't even say a word before she turned around, shrieking and thrusting her hand defensively to her throat.

"It's okay," I said, putting my hands up. "It's just me. Calm—" My sentence was cut short. "Oh my God. Your face!"

She touched the swollen bruise around her eye. "Yeah, I know," she said. "She hit me. She *actually hit* me."

"What? Oh, Becky. I...I'm so sorry. Did you talk to Aaron?"

She nodded. "He was sweet. He was more than sweet actually. I just had to get away. This was the only place I could think of coming."

I nodded, remembering how she always loved escaping here. I just wished she didn't have to escape so often. "You always said you wish she'd notice you."

"I was wrong," she said, a tone of anger rising in her voice through her sadness. "I was so wrong. She just didn't care before, but *this*—this is pure hatred. What did I do to be so unloved?"

"You aren't unloved. I love you, and Aaron loves you. You're a beautiful person, Becky."

"Then where's my happily ever after?" she asked, still with tears in her eyes. "I always envied how you and Aidan had this fairy tale story."

"It's hardly a fairy tale."

"I want a hero galloping to my rescue on a white stallion."

"Maybe a hero doesn't need a white stallion," I said. "Why can't he have...a black mustang?"

She smiled, suppressing a chuckle. "Things used to be different," she said. "No matter how alone I felt, I could always turn to you and Danny."

"You can still turn to me."

"I know," she said, "but sometimes I miss Danny so much more than I admit. Reading his journal has been so hard. It's bringing it all back again. I can't even imagine how hard it is for you to read it."

I touched her shoulder. "That reminds me to tell you why I'm here," I said. "I am having these suspicions we're missing something."

"We're missing a lot," she said. "Like who did it."

I sighed. "You know what I mean."

"Sort of—" She stopped mid-sentence and turned around at the sound of rustling leaves and muffled voices.

"Stay back," she whispered.

She got low to the ground and started inching her way toward where the voices were coming from. I followed behind, seeing two men half hidden behind all the foliage. One was tall and thin with long hair and a baseball cap. The other was shorter with greasy, black hair. As soon as I looked at his eyes, I knew instantly he was the man from the window. My fear and suspicion were immediately replaced by anger, and I narrowed my eyes, feeling a growl rising from the back of my throat.

"What is he doing here?" I whispered harshly. "Do they know?"

Becky furrowed her brow. "Who? Know what?"

"They can't," I said, shaking my head. "How could they?"

"Jane, what are you...?" Becky's voice faded, and her face went pale as she stared at him, recognition washing over her.

I started to stand to my feet, but Becky latched onto my arm, digging her fingernails through my sweatshirt.

"Stop," she hissed. "Don't be an idiot, Jane. Think for a second."

I inched a little closer and heard a twig snap under my foot. I cringed, and the men instantly became alert like blood hounds on a hunt. My entire body started shaking when I saw the black-haired man pull out a knife and those terrible eyes lock on us.

Becky didn't even hesitate before screaming, "RUN!"

I took off as fast as I could, but she still ended up in front of me. Her long stride was eating up the ground as I struggled to keep up. She turned around and ran back to me.

"What are you doing?" she yelled. "Run faster!"

My chest was already burning. "I'm running as fast as I can."

"Damn it. It isn't fast enough!" She pushed me forward, and I picked up my pace, making it up the hill and to the car. She stepped on the gas and peeled out, throwing me into my door. I grunted and pulled my seat belt on. My hands were shaking so badly I couldn't buckle it and soon gave up. Becky pulled over to another side of the river and hid the car behind some trees. My heart was pounding as the images replayed. All I could think about was the knife. The Sevren *were* behind this after all.

"Jane..." Her voice trailed off as she pointed to the tracks leading away from the river. I stared for a moment, noticing they matched the tracks left at her house the night we were being watched.

"My God," I murmured. "So what are you waiting for? Let's get out of here!"

I saw her slowly shake her head as she inhaled deeply. I nodded, letting her get a hold of herself before asking her to drive straight. The knife kept flashing through my memory, causing me to practically start panting.

"Becky, we need to get out of here. We can't stay."

She shook her head again. "No," she answered, slightly out of breath. "Think about it. Staying here is the last thing they'd expect."

"No," I retorted. "No, Becky, please. We can't stay here. They're after us."

"If we leave, they will just come looking for us," she answered. "If we don't leave and they look for us, then we are here alone."

I shook my head mechanically.

"This is our last chance," she said dramatically. "You said Danny was hiding something. Do you think that's why they're here?"

I shook my head. "It can't be. They couldn't possibly know what was in Danny's journal."

"Maybe they just thought they wouldn't be seen. It's usually empty when I come out here."

"Yeah. That's probably it."

"Well, either way, this is our last chance to find it."

"It can't be," I said. "There's another way."

"Jane, you and I both know that isn't true."

I huffed. *There has to be.*

"Unless you want to tell Ai—*him*, then you know this is the only way."

I slammed my fist into the door of the car.

"Damn," I grumbled. "Fine. He hinted at something in his journal," I said. "The tree that grew into the shape of a heart and the metal tin he called his treasure box."

I cautiously got out of the car after her. She turned to look at me, making sure I would follow. I could almost see a sense of panic wash over her eyes just before she started striding down the hill. I followed, still nervous we were being watched. She skillfully swung her legs over some shrubbery, still looking around for anything suspicious, and continued hastily down to the bank. We stopped in front of a small outlet of water about four feet across with no way of getting around it save for a branch that was conveniently placed and hanging down beside Becky. She slowly leaned over the water, placing both hands on the branch, and pushed down on it to make sure it could support her weight. When the branch didn't give, she swung her legs over, clearing the water by no more than an inch. She breathed a sigh of relief as I stood there, shocked at how easily she did that.

"Becky?" I murmured. "Becky!"

I grunted and pulled myself onto the branch. Becky turned around, snickering at the sight of me lying on my belly, trying to figure out how to get the rest of the way over, my feet dangling only inches away from the ice cold water.

"Only you, Jane, would be playing around when there are lives in danger."

"Yeah. Real funny. How about rather than sarcasm, you put that mouth to good use and tell me how to get across this damn thing."

Laughing, she told me to swing my leg over and use my body for momentum. I landed barely on my feet and instantly kept moving farther down. I tightly gripped Becky's arm when I saw a tree across the way.

"Jane, what is it?"

"That's it!" I yelled. "That's the tree."

"What tree?"

"The tree Danny mentioned in his journal. It looks like a heart. That has to be where it is." I sighed. "Of course it has to be on *that* side of the river."

"Well, he couldn't make it easy," she said.

"Do you happen to have a canoe in your pocket? Because otherwise we can't get across."

"Well, you can at least take the paddle out of your butt."

I rolled my eyes.

"There are rocks," she said. "We can get across."

"If our legs were six feet long."

Becky knelt down to start untying her shoes. "Where's your sense of adventure?"

"Becky, are you crazy?" I yelled. "I'm not crossing *that*! There are rapids!"

She started moving across the rocks. She turned to look at me only to see me staring back at her incredulously like she'd lost her mind.

"Um…are you coming?"

"No!" I blurted out. "You're crazy!"

"The clue is over *there*," she said, pointing across the way.

I sighed heavily. Whatever clue was over there was one Danny died for. I had no choice.

I took off my shoes and followed Becky over the rocks. I made my way over to her only to slip, dunking one foot into the freezing water. I pulled my now soggy leg out, staring daggers at Becky. I followed behind until we got to a point where the water was too wide to cross, and minor rapids were gushing by.

"We can't cross this," I said.

Becky pointed to a branch. "What do you call that?"

"Um…a stick."

"Don't be so dramatic," she said. "It's a log—our log, and we're going to use it."

"Becky, that's not a log. It's a tree branch."

Squatting down on the ledge, she plunged her leg into the water, searching for the boulder she could see was submerged. She leaned across the water, using her one leg, the water trying to tear her from her balance and carry her downstream. Inch by inch, she leaned toward the branch and pulled herself onto it.

"Be careful," I called.

She made her way out of the rushing waters and threw her hair back, laughing.

I felt my stomach flip flop as I submerged my legs, looking for the rock, only to be thrown aside. Holding back a scream, I clutched the rocks, trying to catch my breath.

"I don't know if your legs can reach that," Becky called. "You're going to have to use the log all the way across."

Nodding my head, I reached forward, crawling along the branch.

Without warning, it rotated, throwing the lower half of my body into the icy rapids, and I screamed out. Becky squealed and threw herself toward the branch to stabilize it so I could regain my balance. I finally maneuvered myself across and stood beside Becky. She helped me to my feet, chuckling at the pure stupidity of what we were doing.

We continued across, using the remaining rocks. I immediately gave out a groan when I saw the next gap was about seven feet across.

Taking a breath, Becky placed her foot in the water toward another boulder just to slip off. She looked around, refusing to give up.

"Well, now we do need a canoe."

"Yeah," I replied. "Or another stick."

"Ah!" she yelled. "You're a genius."

Turning around, she braced herself, pulling the twenty-foot branch over the seven-foot space. The awkwardness of the weight made it very difficult to maneuver.

"A little help would be nice."

Without missing a beat, I replied, "I'm not qualified to help you. I don't have a medical degree."

Grabbing the branch, I helped her swing it across, barely getting it to hook onto the rocks. Repeating the same careful movements as before, we managed to make it across the water to the boulders at the other side. We jumped from rock to rock and stopped short a foot away from the tree, separated by only a small outlet of water.

"Are you ready?" Becky asked.

"No, but that hasn't stopped me yet."

"Count off," she started. "One…two…three!"

We leapt over the water, onto the bank.

We approached the tree. "What is that?" I questioned, looking at a strange marking on the trunk.

"Looks like some sort of family crest," Becky answered as I ran my fingers over the X-shaped pattern.

"Wonder what the letters mean."

"Initials I'm sure," she said.

"S.K.?"

"Yeah."

"Maybe Magnus isn't his real name," I said, "or maybe those are the initials of the other man."

"Wait," she said. "What was it the detective said?"

"He said there was a tall, thin man with long hair, just like the one we just escaped from."

"Right," she answered. "He never said it was Magnus, did he?"

I shook my head softly and murmured, "S.K." I stopped cold and looked to Becky. "Oh my God!"

"What is it?"

"S.K." I yelled. "Sterling...Keller!"

"Keller?"

I nodded. "That must have been what Danny had found," I cried. "That must have been what he was on to."

"What about the tin?"

I shook my head. "Must be buried by the tree," I said. "You dig here, and I'll start over there."

We started digging. I felt the sting of the icy mud biting into my fingertips and spreading under my nails until I got to what must have been the tin no more than six inches under the mud.

"Becky!"

She crawled over to me. I pulled the tin from the mud, and my memory flashed with pictures of Danny putting his G.I. Joes and baseball inside it. His treasures. It was exactly how I remembered it. It had a soccer ball on the lid, now faded and dirty. I tried opening it, but the lid was rusted shut.

"Here," Becky said. She started pushing the lid off using a rock, and it popped open. Inside was an envelope concealed in a plastic bag to keep it dry. I took it out and opened the envelope. There was a photo of Danny standing beside Keller. Keller had his hand on Danny's shoulder, looking down like a proud father. Danny was staring into the camera almost expressionless but with a hardness in his eyes. Across the photo in bold, red ink, he had written, "BETRAYER!"

It seemed like hours before I could speak. "We were right," I mumbled.

"It wasn't Magnus," she said. "It was Keller this whole time."

"He's trying to re-establish The Sevren!"

"What?" she bellowed, terror creeping into her voice.

"He must be," I continued. "What other reason could he have?"

She shook her head. "I don't know," she murmured, "but let's not make assumptions until we find out more."

I nodded. "That's probably a good idea."

Muddling my thoughts with possibilities was the worst thing that could happen at that point. I had to keep my head clear and my suspicions at bay at least for a while longer.

"There's a letter here," I said. "This should tell us more."

"Read it out loud."

I shook it open and almost gasped at the sight of Danny's familiar hand writing.

"Dear Jane,

If you are reading this, it means something has happened to me. I want you to know that it's all right. I also want you to know how proud I am that you found this letter. I only hope that it isn't too late. If the man in the photo comes to you like I predict he will, do not trust him. He is a member of a secret and evil society called The Sevren and was using me to bring down The Silver Wing, mentioned in my journal, by accusing Magnus of murder. He is the murderer, not Magnus. It doesn't end there. I met a woman from that evil society. I hid my face to avoid being recognized if she decided to betray me later. She told me that she and a friend of hers wanted to leave The Sevren but didn't know how. I appointed the job to myself to help save her and the boy they as well deceived. Unfortunately, I will not have the time to save them. I know that this task will be my last, and I am okay with that. This is why I need you more than ever now, Jane. Finish what I started. Find the one called James. He is one of the good guys. He will help you. I love you.

~Daniel"

My trembling hand drifted up to my open mouth. "Oh my God."

"We need to tell Aidan," she whispered.

I sighed. "I know."

Chapter Ten

"MAYBE HE WAS RIGHT," I said. "Maybe we really shouldn't have kept anything from him in the first place."

"He's gunna kill us," she added.

I turned the corner slowly, terrified to actually reach the coffee shop.

"Did you even call him?"

I shook my head.

"Then how can you be so sure he'll be here."

I almost laughed. "Where else is he ever?"

We walked in, and Aidan wasn't there. We ordered coffee and sat down. The tension was almost unbearable. We couldn't even speak a word to each other.

Becky stared at me for a moment with an accusing look on her face.

"Becky, he'll show up."

"Why don't you just call him?"

I thought that if I were to call him and tell him to meet me here, I would somehow lose my nerve and take off. I figured that if I could stay here long enough and see him in person, he wouldn't let me leave until I told him everything I knew.

"Please?" she asked. "Just call him. I can't sit here like this all day."

I groaned and was just about to ask to borrow her cell phone when I noticed Aidan's car pulling up in the parking lot.

"See?" I said, turning toward the window. "I told you he would be here."

"We can't talk here," she said.

I nodded. "I know."

We left our coffee at the table and met him at the door. I didn't say a word to him, just walked back toward my car. He followed.

"Jane?"

"Just follow me," I said. "We need to talk to you."

He narrowed his eyes, and the color drained from his face.

"Okay."

Becky got in the passenger's seat. "My mom isn't home," she said. "We'll have more privacy at my place, and I'm sure Aidan can keep us safe if…something happens again."

I nodded, and Aidan's cherry-red Mustang followed behind me to Becky's house.

We instantly walked into her den, and she locked the window and pulled a dark blanket over the sheer curtains.

"What's going on?" Aidan demanded before any of us had even settled into a comfortable position on the couch.

"You have to promise you won't be mad," I said.

He sighed and ran his hands through his sandy brown hair as I had seen him do when he was frustrated. "I am promising nothing."

"I figured," I murmured.

"We didn't mean any harm," Becky said, "but this case is very personal for us."

"Case?" he spat. "What *case*?"

Nice going, Becky.

"Uh…situation," she corrected.

"Fine. What did you do?"

She looked to me, so I answered. "While I was reading the rest of Danny's journal, I found a clue."

"Which was what exactly?"

"He hinted at something near the river."

He interrupted me there. "Which river?"

"Um…Nasika."

He instantly groaned. "Continue."

"We found a tin can buried in the mud."

He nodded and waved his hand at me to keep going.

"It was Danny's. I remember it from when we were kids. There was a picture and letter inside."

"Do you have it with you?"

I nodded and handed it to him.

"You shouldn't have," he said. "If you found something out, you should have told me. Nasika is not a safe place."

"I know," I answered.

Aidan stared at the letter for a moment before Becky spoke.

"Whatever it is you know, we want to know too," she said.

He glanced up at her, pressing wrinkles into his forehead and instantly averted his gaze back at the letter. "You know how this works," he answered.

"No!" I snapped. "We just told you everything. The *only* way we are going to stop keeping things from you is if you stop keeping things from us."

"Damn. You two are impossible."

"We mean it," I continued. "When you 'need words with people' we want to know what words and what people."

"Fine," he snapped. "Get your shoes on. We're going to talk to Luna."

"Now?"

"Yes," he spat. "Now. And brace yourself—because I'm gunna kill her."

I saw the color slowly drain from Becky's face.

"Oh, relax," he said. "Just a figure of speech."

"They're never going to be gone, are they?" she whispered to me.

"They already are," Aidan hissed. "This is not The Sevren. This is Keller. It isn't the same thing."

I sighed. *But it comes from the same place.*

Driving to Luna's was like a trip back in time. Even the rain softly drizzling over the trees made me feel like I was back in the days when everything was still shrouded in mystery. It made Aidan look so beautiful and innocent to me. I had missed seeing him that way. It was so silent. I could almost hear his breathing. It made me so uncomfortable to know how annoyed he must have been with us.

"Aidan, I'm really sorry," I murmured.

He glanced at me and nodded. "No more of this, okay?"

I knew we had screwed up—again. I didn't even need to answer.

When we got there, nothing felt strange to me anymore. It was very comfortable and familiar. That feeling lasted only until we approached the front lawn, my memory assaulted with visions of the man I had killed in the very grass I stood in. I could still see the look on his face when Luna drove the knife into his back. I could still see the blood pooling out and soaking my shoes after I emptied the entire clip of bullets into his chest. I choked on my breath for a moment before I was able to regain my control. I inhaled deeply and followed Aidan to the door.

"James!" she exclaimed. "What are you do—?"

"Not now, Luna," he growled. "This is not the time for warm greetings!"

Becky and I stepped inside after him without even waiting to be invited. The house looked exactly as I remembered, from the redwood-framed furniture to the finely painted china in the cabinet to the right.

I could see the shock on Becky's face at seeing Luna. I recognized it as the same reaction I had at first seeing someone so beautiful.

"What's this about then?" she asked.

"It's about *this*," he growled, handing her the letter.

"What is…?" She broke off and turned to me. "Wait… What are *you* doing here?"

"I…um…"

"And who is she?" she demanded, pointing at Becky.

"Don't worry about that right now," Aidan said. "How did you do it?"

"Do what?"

"Get us out!" he yelled. "How did you get us out of The Sevren? The *real* story. And why didn't you tell me about this?"

She sighed and turned away. "I didn't tell you because it wasn't important," she said. "I didn't tell you because I was taking care of it."

"Read the letter."

"What?"

"Read it."

She hesitantly opened the letter and began reading. She fell softly onto the couch behind her.

"Oh my God," she whispered. "Where—?"

"Jane found it," Aidan answered, his voice finally calm. "It was her brother, Luna."

Her head instantly snapped up, and she stared at me with her blue eyes huge and full of unshed tears.

"Jane…I'm so sorry. I didn't know."

I nodded, unable to say anything.

"How did you do it?"

"He found me," she said. "He came to me when I was out one evening. He said he could help me."

"Did he say who he was?"

She shook her head. "I didn't even see his face."

"Why would he come to you?"

She shook her head again, and the tears rolled down her cheeks. "He spoke of you," she said. "He told me that you were good and needed to be saved from them."

"You never told me?" he yelled. "Why?"

"I didn't think it was important."

"How could you think that? He said I was good? You never wondered what that meant or where he heard that from?"

"He was a Silver Wing," she said. "I could tell somehow. I could also tell he had people behind the scenes. Someone like Ian perhaps. I don't know. All I know is he knew things that led me to trust him. Knowing about you was the one thing that made me believe him and find Walter like he told me to."

"He was trying to save us, Luna."

She nodded. "I know. I wish he knew he did."

"I'm still completely baffled as to how he knew."

I finally answered his question. "It was Danny's job to know," I said. "He was spying for Keller. I am sure he needed your help."

"Why mine?" Aidan asked.

"Because he knew you were good," I answered. "And he knew you could get information for him. He just needed Luna to convince you."

"That must have been before he realized that he and Keller weren't working for the same team."

I nodded.

"Next time something like this comes to us, you *have* to tell me," he demanded. "All of you have *got* to stop keeping things from me, or everything we have fought for is going to be destroyed."

Luna nodded. "I'm sorry."

Chapter Eleven

THE NEXT DAY was when we had planned on meeting at Becky's. Her mom was out as usual, so we would be alone.

"Where is he?" Becky asked, still wringing her hands together.

"Becky, it's just now two o'clock. Give him a few minutes, and he'll be here."

She just nodded but didn't relax until his knock came at the door.

We perked up and went to answer it.

"I told you it was a terrible idea to get *her* involved," he said, glancing at Becky.

"What's that supposed to mean?" I snapped.

He glared at me without answering. I knew exactly what he meant. She looked completely terrified and anxious through everything that was happening. I never even once saw her express anything less than severe apprehension.

Aidan and I took our seats on the couch in the den. Becky moved aside the blanket she had draped over the window and checked the lock.

"If he comes back—"

"He won't," Aidan interrupted, gesturing for her to sit.

"Yeah, but...if he does..."

"Then I will take care of it, okay? You have nothing to worry about."

She nodded and sat beside me. I could almost hear her heart pounding.

"Okay, first things first," Aidan began. "You said you wanted to finish what Danny started, right?"

"Yes," I answered. "It's more of something I *have* to do than something I *want* to do."

"Yeah, I understand. Maybe you getting involved can work out for the better."

"Would not have expected you to say that," I answered, suppressing laughter.

"Not that it's what I prefer," he said. "But I have an idea."

I stared at him for a moment, trying to read his face.

"What do you mean?" Becky announced. "What kind of idea?"

I realized she had noticed his tone as much as I had. He meant a dangerous idea. I could always tell when he was worried about something.

He sighed before replying. "I need to know something first," he said. He turned to stare at me with his green eyes big and his face rock hard. "And you have to promise to be completely honest with me!"

I put my hands up in defense. "I have told you everything," I said. "I promise."

"Okay, then you have not met Sterling again?"

I shook my head. "No."

"You swear?"

"Yes, Aidan!"

"Okay, then you need to tell me everything that happened that night...in detail."

I told him the entire story, not even leaving out the part about him drugging me.

"Taking candy from strangers, Jane? Really?"

"Like I don't already feel like an idiot," I snapped. "You don't need to make it worse."

"So he said the murders were starting again?"

"What could that mean?" I asked. "According to Danny, he *is* the murderer."

92

"Exactly."

"So what is he up to?"

"That's where you come in."

"Me?" I yelled. "No, Keller wants to kill me!"

"No," he retorted. "He wants a reason to kill Magnus. He knows that if he kills him without reason, he has broken the rules and that there will be hell to pay."

"Why Magnus?"

"Because he is the last leader that stands in Keller's way of creating a new establishment of The Sevren—or whatever he's trying to do."

I groaned. "So he wants me to prove Magnus's guilt."

"Yes."

"Magnus isn't the only one standing in his way," I said. "There is Walter."

He shook his head. "Walter may be a strong man," he said, "but Keller isn't worried about him. Magnus is smarter and more capable than Walter. He's the only one who can really stop Keller."

"Doesn't that mean we need to find him?"

He nodded. "That comes later," he said. "For now, we need to come up with a plan for you. A good place to start is not making the same mistake Danny did."

"What mistake?"

"Letting Keller know you are on to him. What other reason would he have had?"

"I don't like this plan," Becky interrupted. "What if he does want to kill Jane?"

"If he kills her, he can't use her," he answered. "She is no use to him dead."

Becky sighed and started fidgeting with the ruffles of her skirt. "Can you promise me you know what you're doing?" she asked. "That you know she will be safe?"

He nodded. "We have to do this carefully. If all I had to do was take care of Keller, I could do that on my own...but..."

"But?"

"But he has friends—friends who are just as smart and as strong as he is."

"Like the guy from the window?"

He nodded.

I shook my head. "How many friends?"

"I don't know." He sighed. "But enough to need a plan for."

"What do I have to do?"

"Finding Keller is step one," he said. "Setting up a meeting with him and all his friends."

"And then?"

"Leave the rest up to us."

"Us?"

He nodded. "Magnus, Walter, Evey, Ian, and me."

Oh God.

"Another battle, Aidan?"

"Maybe."

"And after him?" Becky yelled. "After him, who else will come after us?"

"I told you already this is not The Sevren. This is Keller. The one radical follower we missed in the massacre of the rest."

"How can you be sure he is the only one?"

"Becky, you shouldn't even be involved!" he yelled. "So the last thing you should be doing is questioning me. You both know that I am the *only* one who can help you."

She huffed and flopped back down.

"If this isn't about The Sevren, then why would Keller be trying to re-establish it?"

Aidan sighed. "Look," he started. "I talked to Walter, and we're beginning to think that may not be his goal."

"What do you mean?" I mused. "What other goal would he have?"

"I don't know. It was Danny who could have told us that. The only other person who knows anything…is Magnus."

"So, we need to find him?"

He nodded.

"How?"

He looked away from me and sighed heavily. I knew that meant that whatever it was he had to tell me was something I wouldn't like.

"Aidan?"

"You won't like it," he snapped, turning back to face me, "but it's the only way."

"What is?"

"Like I told you, we need to set up a meeting with Keller."

I nodded until I processed what he was saying, and I froze.

Aidan raised his hands in defense. "Just relax," he said. "I promise you nothing bad will happen to you, all right?"

"You want—you want *me* to talk to him?"

"Yes."

I wanted to protest and tell him there had to be another way, but it seemed like my voice was caught in my chest, and I couldn't push it out. I wanted all of it to be over. I was stupid to think I could stay safe and uninvolved. With or without Aidan, it had become clear that this was the path my life was meant to take. Like Danny…it was my fate. Still, I found myself shaking my head mechanically when the fear set in.

"No," I murmured.

"What?"

"No, Aidan, I can't."

"Yes, you can," he answered. He took my hands and rested his forehead against mine. "After everything we have been through, I know that you can do anything."

I felt the sting of tears in my eyes and the familiar heat rushing to my face. I didn't want to do this, but I knew I had no choice.

"Is it set up?"

Aidan shook his head. "Not yet. I need to talk to Walter. If Keller gets suspicious, this entire thing could end in disaster."

"Not the best way to convince me this is a good idea," Becky murmured.

He narrowed his eyes and glanced her way. "I am also not trying to convince you."

Becky flopped down on her couch beside me. I grasped her hand but couldn't say anything. There was no way I could help her feel better about anything.

"I think it is safe to say that you stay here," Aidan said,
glancing back at Becky.

"You would say that," she said, "but Jane and I already promised we were in this together."

He immediately stood up and started pacing before responding.

"No," he announced. "There is no way I'm allowing that!"

"She promised."

I could see the anger littering Aidan's features and the fear in Becky's eyes.

"Maybe he's right," I said.

"What?"

"Maybe it's better for you to stay here."

"This is *our* thing, Jane," she whispered, leaning in so Aidan couldn't hear. "It was my idea to even ask him in the first place."

I sighed and started wringing my hands together.

"Please," she begged.

I leaned in a little closer. "Call me," I said in a whisper. "We'll talk about it. But Aidan *can't* know."

"Okay."

"She'll stay," I said to Aidan.

"Good. Now let me talk to Walter, and I'll see you tomorrow."

He left before he had time to realize I was lying.

I never knew how he did half the things he did, but somehow, they always worked out. He was back no more than an hour later, telling me it was set up.

"I don't want to do this," I murmured.

He sat beside me and put his arm around me. "I know," he said. "I don't want this either, but you know this is the only way."

"So what do I do first?"

He smiled. "For starters—breathe."

I nodded. "And then?"

"All you have to do is tell him that you're ready to help him prove Magnus's guilt."

"Which is a flat out lie."

"Well, of course," he answered flatly. "You obviously have to keep that part to yourself."

"Aidan, you know I'm a terrible liar."

He shrugged. "Only because I know you," he said. "Keller shouldn't catch on."

"That's reassuring."

He ignored me and continued. "Ian contacted Keller, masquerading as one of his men. You will meet him tomorrow night at the park."

I remembered Danny's journal entries, and my stomach grew into knots. What if Aidan was wrong and Keller only wanted to finish what he started and kill me?

"What if—?"

"What if nothing," he interrupted. "You will be fine, Jane. You are the only one who can do this."

Any last words of protest sank back into my stomach, and I began to feel nauseated. I really had no choice. I wanted to just curl up into myself and pretend none of this was happening. I wanted it to be over.

"What time?" was the only thing I could choke out.

"Be there by six," he said.

Chapter Twelve

THE PREVIOUS FEAR had very quickly grown into anxiety and anticipation. I almost wanted to meet Keller at that very moment. The sooner I did this, the sooner it would all be over. Becky had agreed to not let herself be seen until we were sure he wasn't going to hurt me.

"What time is it?"

"It's only five," she said. "Relax. We aren't going to be late."

Being late was not my concern. I just wanted to go get it done and behind me.

"We can wait at the park," she said. "If you want to."

I glanced her way and realized the fresh air and coolness would definitely make me feel better. I nodded and pulled on my sweatshirt. The walk was silent, and the surrounding breeze was doing nothing but chilling me through my thin clothing. We stopped at a park bench near the empty swing set and watched the sun go down until the sky was streaked with pink.

Becky nudged me, breaking my attention away from the sunset and to a dark figure standing across the lot.

"Is that him?" she whispered.

"I can't tell," I said. "Should we go over there?"

She shrugged. "It couldn't hurt."

SARA J. BERNHARDT

I got up, and immediately, I felt that fear again, the kind that rises from the pit of my stomach and up into my throat, making me wish it was logical to scream. We walked very slowly, making our way across the lot.

"Stop," Becky hissed, pulling me back until we were hidden behind one of the nearby buildings. "Look. There is someone else there."

I narrowed my eyes in confusion and inched closer to the two dark figures. Becky followed, telling me to keep quiet. I peered through the approaching darkness just enough to see familiar, shoulder-length hair.

"That's Keller," I whispered.

"Is that other guy the one from the window?" I could hear panic rising into her voice. "Jane, this is a setup. We should get out of here now."

I gripped her arm. "No," I spat. "Look."

She moved slightly closer to me and glanced over my shoulder. I felt her breath explode. "Not him."

"No," I said. "But we should still wait until we know what's going on."

We moved even closer until the men were in ear shot.

"What do you mean you know?" I heard in the voice that could only be Keller's.

"I mean what I said," an older voice replied. "I know. What more need I say, Keller?"

"Well, you just gave me the only thing I need," Keller answered.

"What are you talking about?"

"I couldn't break the rules you know," he answered. I could hear venom behind his words. "They would do worse things to me than kill me for breaking them. But now...oh now, I have every reason to end you."

"You wouldn't," he said. "Who's going to believe you?"

I saw him reach into the inside pocket of his jacket and pull something out. "I can easily doctor this," he said. "Make it appear as though you threatened me."

I realized it must have been a small tape recorder.

"It's your voice," he continued. "What more proof do I need?"

100

The other man was silent for a moment. "What do you want?" he asked, his voice low and almost inaudible from where I stood.

"Nothing you can give me," Keller said. He lunged toward the man, and I watched in horror as grunts and pleas erupted from the stranger, but Sterling didn't relent. Whatever he was doing, I couldn't see well enough to make out, and at the time, I was grateful.

I felt Becky grip my shoulder, and I knew immediately that bringing her with me was a mistake. I was supposed to be protecting her. Why did I keep screwing up no matter how much I tried to do the right thing? She didn't need to see this.

"You were right," I whispered. "Let's get out of here!"

We started moving when Keller's voice sliced through the silence.

"Not so fast!" he called.

We turned around to see him only feet away from us.

"We had a meeting, didn't we?"

I was thinking then that it was possible he didn't know what we had witnessed.

I nodded, trying to wipe all expression off my face and force myself to push back the fear and sickness that was swirling through my head. I cleared my throat.

"Yes," I said. "We did."

"I wanted to apologize for Nasika. I didn't know it was you."

"It's fine," I said. It was taking every ounce of composure I had to keep my voice even. If he wanted to kill me, there was nobody there to stop him. I could physically feel my heart pounding and the fear emanating from Becky still standing beside me. I didn't know what to say, and there was a dead body lying only feet away from us somewhere in the dark.

Becky moved behind me and grasped my hand, placing something in it. I realized it was her cell phone. I kept my hand behind my back so Keller couldn't see what I was up to. She wanted me to call Aidan. She was right. He needed to get us out of here.

Before I even had time to figure out what to do, I saw Keller's face twist into anger and felt his fist crash into my cheek. I toppled over, and Becky's cell phone slid across the asphalt. He walked hastily toward it and stomped on it until it cracked into pieces. He turned and stared directly at Becky, who was already whimpering. He grabbed her by the back of her hair and slammed her face into the brick building. She crumpled into a heap on the ground, and blood pooled out around her. I tried to scream, but he held me by my throat.

"You think I didn't know this was a set up?" he growled.

My lungs were begging for air, and my face was burning.

"You think I am stupid?"

I tried to murmur out a response, at least so he would let me go, but I couldn't. Finally, he released me, and my lungs began wrenching coughs from my chest.

"I don't know what you're talking about," I choked out, rubbing my sore neck. "There is no set up."

He hit me again, and the darkness surrounding us dissolved into complete blackness as I fell into unconsciousness.

There was no sight at first, just the smell of kerosene or maybe gasoline that assaulted my nose. I tried opening my eyes when I realized I must have been blindfolded. I could hear voices, but they were muffled as my brain was forcing itself awake. I tried to think straight, tried to remember where I was. That's when all of the memories came over me in a play by play like a bad horror movie, and I remembered Becky. I remembered the image of her splayed on the dirty ground, not moving. Oh God. Why wasn't she moving? Where was she? I felt my body begin to quake, realizing I wasn't alone. Keller was here somewhere with a plan to do more than hurt me. My hands were tied behind what must have been a chair, and I wriggled them to see if I could get free. The bounds were tight, and the more I tried to loosen the knots, the worse the ropes cut into my wrists. I winced and heard the sound of footsteps and the creaking of a door.

"Ah, she's awake," I heard. It was Keller's voice.

"About time," I heard from another man. I didn't recognize the voice but was almost certain it was the man from the window.

"I told you she would be fine," Keller said.

"Yeah, well that isn't always the truth," I heard him chuckle as he replied.

That only reminded me again of Becky and what he did to her. I wanted to scream and lunge myself toward him but forced myself to stay calm to try to think of a way out of this mess.

"I told you that digging around wasn't a safe thing to do," he spat, forcefully wrenching off my blindfold. "It would have been wise to listen to my advice."

The darkness behind the scarf across my eyes only slightly lightened in the dim, dank room as my eyes adjusted to the scene before me. I blinked rapidly, seeing the two men standing over me. I had to reply if I wanted him to keep talking, and I had to know where I was. "I was only doing what you asked," I said. "You wanted me to prove Magnus's guilt, remember?"

"Oh, do you really think I ever needed you for that?" he said. "I knew you were going to set me up, and all I had to do was wait. Magnus is dead now. I killed him myself. Now all I have to do is wait for your boyfriend. He and the old man are the only ones standing in my way now. You will lead them right to us."

I realized that must have been what Becky and I witnessed the night before. "Standing in your way of doing what?"

"Do you know how long I have waited to start my own alliance? An alliance that will end all others? The Sevren and The Silver Wing are responsible for so much death and destruction. It is time we put an end to them and clean up."

"Clean up?"

He chuckled. "Yes. That is why we are here. We are starting an alliance of The Cleaners to keep all others in check."

"Don't you get it?" I yelled, my fury rising with my words. "In trying to stop the existence of cults, you are creating another one? Does that actually make sense to you?"

"Oh, it isn't a cult," he said. "It is an alliance."

"It's a cult," I spat. "An alliance is exactly what The Sevren called itself as well. This is madness. It will never work!"

"We're the good guys here, Jane. We want to end the world of the occult."

"No," I answered, "you want to control it!"

I felt his fist strike my face, and I struggled to regain my composure. I knew what this was all about now. Keller never intended to re-establish The Sevren. He intended to start an entirely new sect and make it strong by putting an end to the ones who would stand up to them. The only ones able, being Aidan, Walter, Evey, and Luna. Of course, Becky and I had to go due to association. As long as the remaining leaders and high ranked members of The Silver Wing were dead, they could not re-gather their forces and stop Keller. And now, Aidan was on his way here to rescue me. He was falling right into Keller's trap. I couldn't let him do that. I had to find my own way out of here before he got too close. I wracked my brain for an idea but was too frightened and confused to think straight. Keller's voice tore me from my thoughts.

"Now I don't want you to scream, Jane."

"What?"

He revealed a huge syringe filled with some kind of clear liquid. Panic immediately struck, making me almost dizzy. I struggled hopelessly with my bounds, feeling the rope cutting into my wrists and ankles, but still I fought.

"Oh, now you're just being silly," he taunted. He stepped forward and plunged the needle into the soft skin on my neck. My vision went dark before I even had time to scream.

Chapter Thirteen

WHEN I CAME TO, it was light that awoke me. It was bright like someone was shining a flashlight directly into my eyes. My vision cleared, and I realized I was glaring into the light of a full moon. I was in a steal cage with one cement wall and a cement ceiling. I was lying on a scratchy cot, barely big enough for me. I stood to my feet just to fall back down when my head began throbbing. I remembered the needle then and wondered what exactly Keller had injected me with. I waited for the headache to ease a bit and stood up again, gripping the cold, metal railing holding me in.

"Hey!" I yelled. "Keller, you bastard!"

I screamed and yelled but heard no reply. I put my head in my hands, hoping it would help to clear my mind. My head was still hurting, and I only felt half awake. Wherever I was, I knew I wasn't getting out any time soon. It took me a few moments of sorting out my thoughts to remember all of the events that led me here, and I remembered Becky. I remembered her on the ground, the blood. I didn't want to think about it. I didn't want it to be real, but somehow, I knew deep down—she was gone. I fell onto the floor and sobbed uncontrollably until I was interrupted. A man came to my cell and opened the door.

"I have instructions," he said. "Get up."

I stumbled to my feet, and he kept his hands on my shoulders as he led me to an upper floor with cement steps. I could feel myself physically shaking with anxiety. I knew that wherever he was taking me I would not want to be. When we arrived at a door, he opened up and pushed me inside. He shut the door behind him.

There was a small desk and a lamp with potted plants and leather furniture. It looked like a small office. I was confused. It clearly had air conditioning and a back room with cubicles. I rubbed my temples to clear my head. A man appeared at the desk. He couldn't have been more than thirty, dressed very professionally in a suit and tie.

"Sit," he told me.

I obeyed and sat in one of the leather chairs.

"Keller tells me you are important."

"Important?" I repeated curtly.

"Yes," he answered. "Very much so."

"Yeah, well, Keller also believes me to know more than I do."

"Oh, I don't think so," he answered. "I know about your brother. He was too smart for his own good. Keller *had* to turn him over to Abraham sooner than he wanted to. He had no choice. Daniel knew too much."

I couldn't respond right away. I let myself process the words.

"What?" I whispered.

"He was only meant for one task, but he found out who Keller really was. Keller couldn't take any chances."

I groaned and began feeling sick. It was him. It was all him. He was the one responsible for Danny's death. I felt a hot rage surging through me. I bared my teeth like an animal, and before I even knew what I was doing, I had hurled myself over the desk and began attacking the man.

He held me down, pinning my arms to my sides.

"Don't shoot the messenger," he demanded. "You need to calm down."

"Calm down?" I yelled. "You are all murderers. I'll kill you!"

He called for help, and another man came by and picked me up by my hair, shoving me back into the leather chair. I tried to fight him off a few times, but he kept pushing me back.

"Sit here and be quiet, or I will beat you."

I knew he meant it, so I sat there, fuming.

"Now, my associate here is going to take you back to your cell until you are ready to cooperate."

The other man grabbed me by my arm and shoved me back down the stairs and into my cage.

"Keller!" I yelled. "Keller, let me out of here!"

"You can scream all you want," I heard from what must have been an adjoining wall. "He won't let you out!"

I jumped, turning to the wall of my cage. "What?"

"There's nothing you can do," the voice said.

"Who are you?" I asked.

"Who are *you*?"

I sighed, wondering if I should say anything. "My name is Jane."

"How do you know Keller?"

Again came the thought of ignoring the question. I had no idea what Keller might be up to, and for all I knew, this person was a spy. I settled for a half truth. "I don't really. It's…a long story."

"Well, we have all time in the world," she started. "I doubt either of us will be getting out of here any time soon."

I couldn't even see this girl's face, so the last thing I was going to do was trust her with anything. "Why don't you go first?"

She chuckled. "I guess I was in the wrong place at the wrong time."

"Meaning what exactly?"

She was silent for a moment. "I don't know how else to put it. What about you?"

"Wrong association," I said.

"Ah. Sounds to me like he may want something from you."

The thoughts of Aidan came back to me. I knew exactly what he wanted. If he wanted to kill Aidan, all he had to do was wait. Even knowing this, I had to know what she was thinking.

"Like what?"

"Oh, well, I don't know," she said. "Maybe information on this 'associate'?"

I hesitated before responding. "What makes you think he believes I will tell him anything?"

She laughed. "Do you expect him to ask nicely?"

"I guess I shouldn't," I said.

"I hope you are tough, Jane."

"What's that supposed to mean?"

"You have no idea what Keller is capable of."

I scoffed, remembering him killing Magnus and my beloved Becky. "I know a lot more than you think."

I thought I heard her sigh but wasn't sure.

"So you still haven't told me who you are," I said.

"Oh, didn't I? My name is Alexandra. Call me Alex."

I nodded, then remembered she couldn't see me. "Okay," I said.

The conversation drifted off after a few more useless remarks. Neither of us were trusting enough to tell the other much of anything. I had to admit to being painfully curious. Who was she, and why, if she was connected to this, had I never met her before? I guessed it made sense that there were people involved who I didn't know of, but all of this seemed to be focused on Aidan and The Sevren. If anyone knew everything about that, it was me.

I decided not to think about it and direct my focus toward how I was going to get out of here. My mind was clouded, yet vivid memories of Becky collapsed on the dirty ground assaulted me. I couldn't think of anything but the pain of losing her. This horrific nightmare had now claimed two of my loved ones, and I knew it was not yet over. I tried to close my eyes and think about something—anything else. I felt almost suffocated as the reality finally set in. Becky was gone. I would never again tell her my secrets or confide in her. I would never again confess my fears and hear her tell me that everything would be okay. I was alone now. Truly alone.

I couldn't stop thinking about all the things I remembered about Becky—the way she always pulled the cuffs of her sweaters over her hands or the way she laughed. I always envied her laugh. It was musical, almost melodic. I let myself break down, and I sobbed until hiccups wrenched from my stomach.

I don't remember falling asleep, but I must have because I was roused by an unfamiliar voice.

"Miss Callahan?"

I turned, groggy, and opened my eyes. I didn't recognize him, but he reminded me of Keller—same long hair, silvered at the temples, same long nose and light brown eyes littered with expressions I could not define. I stared at him for a moment, waiting for him to say something.

"Let's go," he finally said, waving me up with his left hand.

I hesitated, reluctant to obey.

"Now," he spat.

The urgency in his voice forced me up, and I followed him to the door of my cell. He turned to me before stepping through and pulled out a pair of handcuffs.

I sighed. "Are those really necessary?"

He gave me a wry smile. "Are they?" he asked.

"Not at all."

He shrugged. "I'll be nice," he said, tucking the cuffs back inside his jacket, "but don't test me."

I nodded, breaking eye contact and followed him down a vacant, cement hallway. The light was low from the tiny, dirt-caked windows positioned every few feet across the walls, some covered with dark paper. I shuddered at the realization of not having any idea where I was. I could tell it was late morning or afternoon from the tiny bits of sunlight pushing through the crevices of dirt and torn paper coverings, but that didn't ease my discomfort.

I remained silent, following a few paces behind. The man repeatedly turned around to make sure I was still behind him as if he expected me to make a break for it in a hallway with no conceivable way to escape. He stopped abruptly at a steel door. He hadn't even knocked when I heard the lock click, and the door opened slowly.

"Come in," I heard. It was Keller. "Tony, you mind waiting outside?"

"Sir," he replied and closed the door behind him.

"What the hell do you want?" I growled.

"Is that any way to speak to me?" he started. "I let you out of your cage. I thought you would be thankful."

"Right. Since you're the one who put me in there in the first place, forgive me if I am a little reluctant to thank you for anything." I bit my tongue to refrain from mentioning Becky. Accusing him out loud would cause me to lose my temper completely, and I couldn't risk it.

He chuckled dryly. "Have a seat," he said, gesturing to a chair in front of a redwood desk.

"I'd rather stand," I said, crossing my arms in front of my chest.

"Jane, just sit down."

I wasn't in the mood to argue, so I took the seat and stared at my hands in my lap.

"Now, I am going to ask you some questions, and you will answer them honestly."

I scoffed. "Really? Let's test that theory."

"I don't have time for games," he said sternly.

"Well, I'm not playing any."

"You will answer my questions or else you will be punished. I don't have to ask nicely."

I shuddered, remembering what Alex had said. Keller wanted to know where Aidan was. He wanted to kill him. How much would he put me through before I broke? How much pain could I endure? I tried to hide my discomfort before making eye contact. He would strike at any sign of weakness. I couldn't let him see it. He stood up and walked around the desk so he was right beside me.

"I can't have you fighting with me, Jane," he whispered in my ear. "Do I have your cooperation?"

I didn't answer. I was too focused on trying to ignore the way he made my skin crawl.

"Don't make me ask you again." I could hear the urgency in his voice and managed a feeble nod.

He leaned back and sighed. "Good. So where is your boyfriend now?"

I knew he was going to ask this, but even as he did, I felt the familiar feeling of shock. "What?"

"You heard me," he said. "Where is Aidan Summers?"

He called him Aidan, which caused another feeling of surprise to wash over me.

"I don't know," I said. It was the truth. Knowing Aidan, he could be anywhere.

"Don't lie to me."

"I'm not lying," I said. "I really don't know where he is. He's better at hiding than anyone." I swallowed, hoping that was true. I had several ideas of where he might be but wasn't willing to give up any of it.

Keller sighed and returned behind his desk. He opened a drawer and retrieved something.

"I need you to be honest with me."

"I am being honest."

He chuckled quietly, shaking his head. He came up behind me again, and I felt the stab of a needle in the back of my neck. I gasped. Damn.

"Now, we are going to try this again."

I felt my head become cloudy, and my vision blurred. I tried to keep my eyes open for fear of passing out again. My entire body felt like it weighed a thousand pounds, and I didn't have the strength or energy to move.

"Now, where is Aidan?"

I was so confused it took several minutes for the question to process.

"Ai—" I tried to say his name, but my voice faded, and I couldn't force the words from my mouth.

I felt Keller strike me hard across my face. I cried out and instantly became more aware of where I was. The fog momentarily lifted long enough for me to choke out one word. "Aidan."

"Yes!" he spat. "Where is he?"

"Why ask me where you are?" I looked at him, seeing Aidan staring back at me with his lucent green eyes. "Are you playing a trick on me, Aidan?"

Keller looked at me, pulling his eyebrows together, looking once again like himself.

"Tony!" he yelled.

The door opened, and the man who escorted me stepped inside.

"Sir?"

"What is this?" he asked, holding up the syringe.

"It's what you asked for, Sir. Is there a problem?"

He gestured to me, but I could barely focus on the rest of what they were saying. I only picked up pieces.

"What? That's too much."

"Quaternary ammonium salts."

"She's not asleep. What else was in it?"

The rest was muffled, and I felt myself slipping into unconsciousness.

I felt Keller shake me. "No," he snapped. "You will stay awake and answer my questions. Where is Aidan?"

I looked into his eyes again, having lost all sense of where I was and who he was. I said the one thing I was trying not to say.

"Why ask me?" I started. "Luna is the one he always goes to when he is in trouble."

It fell out of my mouth, and as it did, I knew it was the wrong thing to say. It was like something inside me had forced the words from my mouth, and I couldn't stop them.

"Luna?"

I was nodding off, and I felt him shake me one last time before I fell into a deep sleep.

I awoke back in my cell—big surprise. My head was still cloudy, but I knew where I was. I remembered what I said about Luna, wishing it was just a bad dream. He would find all of them now—Aidan, Walter, and Luna. He would kill them all, and it would be my fault. I had to think of a way to fix it.

"It won't stop," I heard Alex say from behind the wall.

"What won't stop?"

"The questions," she said. "The drugs."

"What did he inject me with?"

"I don't know," she answered. "Sometimes they sedate us. Other times, they give us things to confuse us or make us hallucinate. From my experience, they combine a lot of different things for different purposes."

"Why?"

"To control us."

"They can't control us if we're dead."

She scoffed. "Yeah, well they obviously don't care if we die."

"They would if they wanted answers."

"Keller doesn't want to kill anyone anyway."

"What?" I interrupted. "Are you crazy? He wants to kill those standing in his way. He told me himself."

"No. He doesn't. He wants to control them. That's what he is doing up there in that lab with those men."

"What lab? What men?"

"There is another floor with a lab. They are up there experimenting with drugs and medications to find the perfect substance to use for mind control."

"Mind control?" My voice swelled with sarcasm.

"I'm serious," she said. "With enough chemicals in your body, it may not only confuse you. It can permanently damage your brain and your thought process. If you forget who you are, they can re-create you."

"How do you know this?"

"Because I've been there."

"Why?"

"You'll find out soon enough."

"Don't do that to me!" I shouted. "Tell me what will happen to me. It happened to you, so you must know."

"I don't," she said, her voice remaining calm even through my shouting. "It's not the same for me as it is for you. What they did to me was designed for me. You will have a different plan."

I sighed and pressed my fingers into my temples, trying to process what she was telling me. I was going to be experimented on, tortured, and, most likely killed. There *had* to be a way out of this.

"We have to get out of here," I said.

"Good luck with that."

Chapter Fourteen

ONCE AGAIN, the morning came as soon as I had fallen asleep. It took a moment for me to remember what had happened, but once my brain found the path, I hunched over, dizzy and sick. There was a bowl of food on the floor beside the bed. It was nothing more than gray mush. I was almost afraid to eat it. I had no idea what Keller might have done to it. I downed the glass of water that was also set on the floor and tried to ignore the knotting in my stomach.

The man called Tony entered my cell again.

"Come on," he said. "Mr. Keller wants to see you again."

"Please," I pleaded, feeling the fear creeping into my chest. "I don't want to go. I don't feel well."

"I'm not asking," he said. He grabbed me by the neck of my long-unwashed shirt and pushed me out of my cage. I choked for a moment and regained my composure. He handcuffed me this time and dragged me through the familiar halls. I fought the urge to cry and struggle, knowing that would only make things worse. He shoved me into Keller's office. Keller was sitting behind his desk again. Tony closed the door on his way out.

"I see he used the handcuffs this time," he said. "Did you put up a fight, Jane?"

I shook my head. "No."

"Well, you don't look too banged up, so I guess you didn't. We do need to get you a shower and a hair brush though. I will make sure it's taken care of."

I just nodded, staring at my hands in my lap, refusing to look up. I could physically feel the dirt on my face and the mats in my hair. For Keller to have said something made me only feel filthier and disgusting.

"We have a bit of a problem."

"Do we?"

He chuckled synthetically. "I sent some men to find this Luna you spoke of, and it's clear she does not exist."

I almost felt my breath explode in relief. "I was confused," I said. "You drugged me. I had no idea what I was saying. I don't even know someone named Luna."

"Well, that I know to be a lie," he said, "and you really need to stop lying to me, Jane. It will only make things worse for you!"

I shook my head, realizing there was nothing I could say that would change his mind.

He got up from his desk and came to stand beside me. He handed me a bottle of water. I looked at him for a moment, wondering if it was really water he was giving me. I took it but didn't even unscrew the cap.

"Take these," he said, handing me two, white tablets.

I shook my head and dropped the pills on the desk.

"Remember I don't have to ask," he said. He revealed a syringe, and I instantly cringed at the thought of him plunging it into my neck. "Your choice."

I could feel the sting in my eyes, and my throat grew tight. I refused to let myself cry. I wouldn't give him that satisfaction. I picked up the pills and plopped them in my mouth. Keller lunged toward me covering my mouth and nose.

"Swallow!" he demanded.

The pills fell down my throat and stung my mouth. Keller let go, and I instantly started choking. He handed me the bottle of water, but I smacked his hand away.

"Suit yourself," he said.

He waited until I was breathing regularly before starting with the questions again.

"We know that Aidan is smart," he said. "Meaning he must not have told you everything. However, I am also smart, Jane, and I can tell when I'm being lied to. Therefore, I will give you one more chance to tell me where he is."

"I. Don't. Know!"

He struck me across my face, and I choked on my breath. It was then I felt the effect of the drugs. My head became cloudy again, and I wasn't sure anymore of where I was. My mind brought me back to other places, to my mom's, Ethan's, Becky's, even Books by the Bay. I was dizzy and frightened. I had to ask where I was, but when Keller answered, I swore it was Aidan.

"What do you mean where are you?"

"I mean, where are we?" I repeated. "I don't remember coming here."

I saw Aidan shaking his head. Another voice joined the discussion.

"Everything is fine, Jane."

I looked over and almost fainted from shock at the sight—of Danny.

"Danny?" My voice was no more than a whisper.

He smiled, and it instantly tore me out of my delusions. It wasn't possible. Danny was dead. It was the one thing I was always sure of. Aidan's face billowed away, leaving only Keller standing there. I started screaming and ran for the door. Keller grabbed me by my shoulders and told me to calm down. I pushed him off me, and in a state of dizziness, I tumbled to the floor. I could feel his hands pressing into my chest. His fingers had grossly elongated claws, and he dug them into me. I screamed and kicked. The pain seared through me as he widened the wounds to submerge his entire hand into my body. I felt the warmth of blood as it flowed out of my open chest, onto the floor around me. I could still move through the pain and continued to fight.

"Jane, calm down," he pleaded. "I'm not going to hurt you."

I knew he was lying. I felt the ripping of his nails as he continued to pull me apart. My very heart was aching, and I knew it would only stop when he succeeded in ripping it out of me. I screamed louder, an odd feeling of emptiness in my chest as if it were opening farther as he would have it do—opening so he could remove my heart while it was still beating. His hands explored my insides, and his sadistic smile was the only thing worse. I didn't stop fighting—I couldn't. I screamed until my throat hurt and kicked and flailed, trying with all my strength to throw him off of me. I realized then, it didn't matter. I was going to die whether he stopped or not.

I felt the familiar prick of a needle in my arm. My body became tired. Even as I tried with all my strength to fight him off, I could feel myself slipping away.

I awoke back in my cell with another throbbing migraine.

"Jane?"

My eyes sprang open, ready to fight when I realized it was just Alex.

"Was that a dream?" I asked.

"I could hear you screaming all the way down here," she said. "I thought he was killing you."

"He was trying," I said. "Or…I think he was."

I examined my body, noticing red finger marks on my upper arms, but my chest was clear of any markings at all. Not even a scratch where I was sure he had thrust his hand through. I whimpered, tearing at my shirt.

"I…I was sure…"

"It's just the drugs," she said. "I told you. It won't stop."

"No," I argued. "No, this was real. The pain, the blood…"

"It's only going to get worse."

Finally, the tears fell. "It's not possible. It had to be…" I paused, searching for the right words. "I don't understand. I was there…in this room. He attacked me. He tore through me like it was nothing. He wasn't exactly himself. He was like…like a monster."

I heard myself and knew I must have sounded completely insane. Alex didn't respond.

"We have to do something," I said. "We have to get out of here."

"That isn't possible. You need to relax. Crying will only make things worse."

"Worse than what?" I shouted. "My best friend is dead, and even if it's in our head, he is still torturing us. I swore he was opening me up to cut out my heart. I could feel it the same as anything else. We have to stop it."

I heard her sigh. "For you to believe it was real only means they are getting closer to whatever they are trying to do."

"You mentioned a lab."

"Yes."

"How long has it been since you were there?"

There was a moment of silence before she replied. "I don't know. I never know what time it is—what day it is."

"I don't want to go there."

"No," she said. "You don't, but I don't think that's an option. I doubt they would take me up there and not you."

I could feel the tears stinging my eyes but really didn't want to let myself break down.

"It's not going to stop."

I shook my head. "When I'm drugged like that, I am not functional."

"I don't have all the answers either, Jane."

"Well, why aren't they torturing you?"

"They did," she said, "for weeks. It's only a matter of time before they take me back up to that office—or worse, the lab."

"And there is nothing we can do?"

"No. There isn't."

I couldn't believe that. She had given up too easily. I couldn't stop fighting. I couldn't let Keller continue to torment me to death or kill Aidan. I had to think of a way to outsmart him. After what I had been through, I knew I was strong enough. All I had to do was stay calm. I had to try and keep my thoughts off Becky, off the overwhelming urge to tear him apart for what he did to her. Staying calm was the only way.

The day dragged on, and again, Tony came to bring me out of my cell. I got up immediately to follow him down the hallway, so he didn't use the handcuffs. He led me down a different hallway around the corner from Keller's office and into another room. There was no door, just a walkway and a corner. Around the corner was a set of three shower stalls. There were no mirrors, but there were small sinks and a counter. Tony laid out some clothing.

"I'll wait outside," he said. "Put these on when you are done. Ten minutes and then I come in to get you."

He rounded the corner, but I was afraid to get undressed, worried there might be cameras or that he would come in anyway just because he could. I only had ten minutes, so I tore off my clothes and rushed to get into the shower as fast as I could. There was only bar soap and a shampoo dispenser attached to the wall. I washed quickly, but slow tears still fell, thinking about Becky and fearing what they would do to me. There were no towels, so I had to pull the uncomfortable polyester clothing over my wet body and let my hair drip down my back, making me feel even colder. I shivered and wrapped my arms around my torso.

I came back to where Tony stood. He glanced at his watch, looked at me, and huffed. He pushed me forward. Keeping his hands on my shoulders, he led me down another vacant hallway with the same tiny, dirty windows. We reached a long flight of metal stairs.

"Up," he demanded.

I stepped onto the first step and heard the metal reinforcements creak under my weight. I gripped the railing and continued. After about ten minutes, my legs started to ache. I tried to ignore my tired muscles and climbed and climbed until we reached the floor. I almost collapsed from lack of energy. Tony smoothed back his long hair. I could hear he was out of breath and hoped that meant we could rest. It didn't. He put his hands back on my shoulders and led me to another steel door.

I inhaled, trying to brace myself for the new horror of the day. My mind played through all sorts of ideas—from the possibility I was entering an interrogation room to the thoughts that maybe it was a torture chamber with dead bodies still hanging from the ceiling.

My throat tightened as I stifled what might have been a scream. Tony rapped twice on the door, and it creaked open. It wasn't Keller on the other side but another, younger man dressed in a bright white lab coat. He looked friendly but not enough for me to ignore the obvious tension and uncertainty behind his eyes. I wasn't stupid enough to trust anyone. He opened the door farther, just enough for me to see this must have been the lab Alex had mentioned. There were white counters with vials and beakers of clear liquid. Some were filled with what looked like blood samples. There were a lot of strange instruments and sharp objects that made me cringe to look at, and everything smelled of disinfectant. There were about seven men in white lab coats, some with face masks, opening and closing labeled drawers.

I tried to glue my feet to the floor, but Tony shoved me in. I bumped into one of the counters, causing the jars and bottles to shake. A few men gasped and turned around, making sure I hadn't spilled anything. I flushed and kept my eyes on the clean, white floor. Everything was quiet except for a few rhythmical beeping sounds. I just stood paralyzed, unsure of what I was supposed to be doing. I turned around to see that the door was shut, and Tony was gone. Two of the men in the lab coats approached me and immediately latched onto my arms. This time I struggled. I screamed and kicked and flailed. Even as I feared feeling the stick of a needle, I didn't relent. The men were silent, only huffing and grunting when I managed to break free for a fleeting moment. There were more hands on me in seconds, and I pulled myself the other direction as hard as I could, screaming as loud as my lungs allowed. I felt my head yanked back by my hair, and finally someone spoke.

"We can't give you the drugs," one of the men said. "We need you lucid for this, so you need to relax. We won't hurt you if you calm down. If you fight, we will have no choice."

I wouldn't have believed him no matter what he said, so I continued to fight, and sure enough, my hair was pulled on even harder until I could feel it being ripped from my scalp, and the fingers dug into my arms until my muscles contracted. One of them struck me hard across my face until I screamed at them to stop. I relaxed involuntarily, too exhausted and sore to continue. I shut my eyes, trying to prepare myself for what was to come next. My mind assaulted me with horrible, gruesome images of being dismembered or surgically altered. I felt the heat and trembles of fear come over me and started fighting back again, no longer feeling the pain in my tired muscles.

"Can't you just sedate her?" I heard a husky voice choke out as he struggled to hold on to me.

"No," another man spat back. "They want her clear headed."

I knew that meant whatever they were going to do I would be awake through all of it. I wouldn't be surprised to be cut open and dissected like a dead lab rat. I started screaming until someone clapped a hand over my mouth. I tried to make my body heavier and scrambled for the door. They pulled me back again, tearing more of my hair out by the roots. I could feel their blows and hear their threats, but I didn't care. I kept struggling. I heard loud, angry footsteps approaching me.

"NO!" I heard the husky voice call out. "No. Roger, don't!"

I felt a crashing pain spread through my head and neck. My eyes closed even as I tried to keep them open. My body fell limp, and the voices around me muffled until I slipped out of consciousness.

When I awoke, my wrists and ankles were strapped to the corners of a flat, white table. I could feel the hard metal pressing against my spine. My head was still throbbing, and I knew that now that I was awake, the torture would begin. I tried to imagine myself somewhere else, but the fear was so intense that my mind kept bringing me back to all the horrific ideas of what they could do to me.

"We are an hour behind schedule," I heard that familiar, husky voice shout. "Next time I tell you not to drug a patient or, in this case, bash one unconscious, you will obey, or rash actions will be taken."

"Sir," I heard in response.

I squeezed my eyes shut, hearing the shuffle of people approaching the table. I squirmed just enough to test how tightly I was strapped down. I could hardly move at all. I held my breath and gasped at the feeling of something freezing on my chest. I opened my eyes to see a man had spread some clear goo over my skin. It looked like it was shimmering, and my skin felt so cold it was going numb. The cold soon led to a burning sensation, and I quietly whimpered.

"It's cold," I whispered.

Nobody answered.

"Really," I pleaded. "Please, take it off. It's so cold. It hurts!"

I started trying to move, but the bounds just dug into my wrists, causing my whimpering to increase.

"Roger," I heard from that familiar voice, "that will do."

I felt the warm dampness of a towel wiping at the sensitive skin of my chest, removing the substance that was by then eating away at me.

I sighed in relief but could still feel a lingering, tingling sensation that made me uncomfortable. The fear and panic started returning when I realized that was just the beginning of what they were planning to do. I tried to close my eyes, tried to pretend I was asleep or somewhere else, but every time I did, I was terrified of not preparing myself for who and what was coming to me next. I couldn't stop myself from glancing around the room and listening intently for any clue of what was impending.

Another man in a lab coat approached me with a vile of some clear liquid. I turned my face away in case he was going to force me to swallow it.

"This won't hurt," he said, "but you have to stay still."

I could feel myself starting to shake with fear, and my insides felt cold as ice. He took a small eye dropper and dripped tiny amounts of the liquid onto my forehead. It felt cold at first but heated up after a few moments. He wiped at my face with a towel and stared down at me.

"How do you feel," he asked me.

I didn't answer.

"I think it's too watered down," I heard him call to someone across the room.

"I'll run a test on it," I heard. "I will give you another sample after I am finished."

He walked away for moment but returned again at my side. He placed a warm, white towel over my face. I jerked my head around, trying to get it off.

"Stop that," he said, but his voice was gentle. "It's for your own good. If you fight, you will only make all of this worse."

I was so sick of hearing that. I knew it was true. Fighting would either get me hit or stuck with another needle. As much as I didn't want to face what they were doing, I would rather not be under again. I felt a strap constrict over my forehead, securing my head to the table. When I gasped, I thought I heard a nearly almost silent laugh from the man behind me. The binding was hard and uncomfortable.

"I'm placing something in your mouth," one of the men said to me. "You wouldn't want to bite off your own tongue, now would you?"

What? I tried to ask but couldn't get the words out.

He stuffed a rubber gag into my mouth. It tickled the back of my tongue, activating my gag reflex. I lay there heaving and trying not to cry.

"Stay still. This may be uncomfortable."

I heard a sharp cracking sound, and my body instantly convulsed. I felt as if my insides were being burned from the inside out. My body involuntarily heaved and seized. I stiffened as best I could, trying to suppress the thrashing. It only made my muscles even more sore and strained. I clenched my teeth into the gag even as I tried not to. I could hardly breathe through the burning pain. I couldn't think about anything but the pain but somehow still wondered what the hell they were doing to me. Did they do this to Alex too? It felt like hours I lay there, suffering, burning…dying.

When it stopped, I felt an indescribable amount of relief, but my body still felt scorched. I felt the gag being removed from my mouth.

"Who are you?" I heard.

"What?"

"Your name. What is it?"

"J-Jane."

"All right. That will do," he said. "Roger!"

I felt that needle prick into my arm, and I could hear myself begging and fighting against it as I felt myself slipping away.

When I awoke, it felt like weeks or even months had passed. How long had I even been here in this place? How long had I been starved and tortured? It could have been days; it could have been months. It was always dark, and I was fed at odd intervals if you could even count what they gave me as food. My eyes were so heavy, but I forced my body awake, willing myself to stay focused on thinking of a way out. After mere seconds, I realized that it was hopeless. There was no way out. I would die here. I tapped lightly on the wall.

"I'm here," I heard Alex say. Her voice was soft and sad.

"How many times have you been up to that lab?" I asked her.

"I don't know," she said. "I lost count."

I felt myself shudder. "What did they do to me?"

"I already told you. It's different for everyone."

"How do you know that?"

She sighed. "Because I have heard others," she said, "their screams and their complaints."

"Others?"

"Yes."

"Alex…was there someone in this cell before me?"

She didn't answer.

"Alex?"

"Yes," she retorted. "Yes…there was."

I felt my body start to tremble, and I wrapped my arms around my body as if to keep myself together.

"What happened to them?"

"I don't know," she said. "One day, he was just gone."

"That's it?"

"Just gone," she repeated.

"Did Keller…?" My voice trailed off.

"I am sure he's dead. To answer your unasked question, yes. I think Keller murdered him—just like he will murder us unless we can get out."

"Alex, there is no way out," I said.

"I thought you didn't lose hope."

"Well, you were right before," I said. "It's hopeless."

"Maybe not."

"What do you mean?"

"When I was in the lab last time, I took something."

"What are you talking about?"

"They put tiny tacks in my skin. All over me," she started. "It was

125

very uncomfortable, and I am not sure why they did it, but when they went to take them out, they left one in the back of my arm."

"A tack?"

"Yes. Like a prong."

I tried not to think about her being stuck with pins, but the image still found its way into my head.

"And?"

"And…" she started, "and…well…I think I can pick the lock on my cell door."

"What? How?"

"The locks are simplistic," she said. "When I get out, I can get you out."

"How will we get past the guards?"

"I haven't figured that part out yet."

I nodded, though she couldn't see me. "Okay, well that's going to be tricky."

"Give me some time, and I'll figure something out."

"Is there a shift switch?" I asked.

"Well, yes," she answered, "but even if the door is unguarded for a few minutes, there are always people around. We would have to be very careful."

"Maybe that's enough time," I said. "Maybe we can go unseen."

"No," she said, "they will see us if we escape. All we need to do is run fast enough and make it close enough to civilization where they wouldn't risk being seen themselves."

"Oh. Is that possible?"

"Anything is possible," she said with a smile behind her words.

For the first time since being in this horrible place, I felt the sputtering feeling of hope in the pit of my stomach, making me almost want to break out in laughter. I tried to calm my nerves. I couldn't let myself believe too much in what Alex was saying. It was too much to hope for too soon. The thought of going back to that lab made me sick, but thinking about all the happiness of an escape would be worse to focus on. If it were to go wrong, then things would be even worse than they already were.

"I can't go back there," I said. "I can't. They'll kill me."

"They won't kill you," she said. "At least not yet. Keller still wants to use you. He hasn't given up yet."

"When can we get out of here?" The urgency in my voice was growing to panic.

"You need to try to be patient as best you can."

"Alex, I cannot go back to that place."

"I know," she whispered. "I know. I'm terrified of being dragged back there just as much."

"Can we get out before they take us up there again?"

She hesitated before responding. "I don't know."

Chapter Fifteen

I WAS startled awake by the sound of shuffling feet and muffled pleading. I opened my eyes and saw who must have been Alex being dragged away by the man called Tony, the same man who forced me up to the lab. She was fighting and scrambling to get free. I wanted to scream, to yell, to try to help somehow, but I froze. My eyes filled with unshed tears. I could hardly breathe knowing what could be done to her. I only hoped she would survive. I felt my stomach drop when I heard the same shuffling of feet only minutes later. He was back. He approached my cell and grabbed me by my hair, shoving me toward the stairs.

"Up," he demanded.

My chest tightened, and I had to force the tears away. Whatever was coming could only be worse. I tried to stop the horrific images in my head. I inhaled deeply as I headed up the metal stairs, feeling the cramping in my legs. I barely even had the energy to stay on my feet. It took everything I had not to topple over down the steps.

We approached the door to the lab. Tony shoved me in and closed the door. I stood, paralyzed. I didn't even have time to think before I felt myself torn from the floor and carried away toward the other side of the room.

I cringed when a horrible scream echoed through the room. My God.

Alex! What were they doing to her? Her cries brought the adrenalin rushing through my limbs. I started fighting as hard as I could, kicking and screaming.

"Alex!" I called. "Alex, I'm here! Don't give in!"

She screamed again, but I knew she heard me.

I felt the impact of a fist crashing into the side of my face. I groaned.

"Stop," the man demanded. "I can't sedate you. You know by now that fighting only makes it worse."

Two other men and a woman in lab coats approached us and followed to what must have been a bathtub. It was old fashioned with claw feet and wasn't hooked up to anything. I started struggling again and was shoved into the tub. It was filled with ice, and I screamed at the shock to my body. I tried to climb out, but the other three people pinned me down, submerging me farther into the agonizing cold.

"Please! Enough!" I begged. "It's killing me! Please!"

"Where is he?" the man holding my shoulders down shouted in my face. "Where is Aidan Summers? Tell me!"

"I don't know! I told you I don't know!"

They continued holding me down until my screams drowned out Alex's.

It was probably early the next morning when Tony came back into my cell. He didn't say a word before handcuffing me.

"Please," I begged. "Don't take me back there."

He gripped my shoulder and pushed me forward. "Walk," he demanded.

I felt hot tears stream down my face as he brought me back to those metal stairs and forced me up. My muscles were already burning after only a few steps. He pushed me again, causing me to stumble. I placed my hands on the step in front of me to regain my balance and stood back upright. I walked as quickly as I could, not wanting him to shove me again. When we reached the top, I felt so tired I wasn't sure I could keep moving.

"I need a second," I said. "Please."

"We don't have time for that," he hissed. "Inside. Now."

He opened the door to the lab and ushered me in. A familiar man, whose name I had never learned, grabbed my arm and led me to a chair.

"Sit," was all he said.

I hesitantly sat down, afraid of what was coming but also relieved to be off my feet. He pushed at the chair, and it leaned back. I gasped at the sudden movement and found myself staring at a ceiling light. The man loomed over me and shined a tiny flash light in my eyes.

"Where are you?" he asked me.

"What?"

"Do you know where you are?"

"I'm in a lab?" I said.

"Good. Do you know how old you are?"

"Eighteen."

"Do you know anyone by the name of James West or Aidan Summers?"

Back to this again. I couldn't lie. I knew what they would do to me if I did.

"Y-yes."

"Good. Now you are going to tell me where to find him."

"I swear to you I don't know," I said. "He is probably dead."

"And why would you say that?"

"Because I haven't heard from him," I lied, "not for a very long time."

"If you are lying to me, you will be sorry," he said. "Can I trust you?"

"Yes," I answered.

"Uh huh."

I suddenly felt his fist crush my cheek, and I yelped loudly.

"Keller told me you would lie."

"I'm not lying. I don't know where he is."

"Don't make me use the serum," he said.

"Serum?"

"Yes. It will make you tell me anything I want to know."

Oh God. Aidan would be caught if I said anything.

He pricked me in the arm again with a needle, and I started screaming and thrashing. I tried to run, but he pushed me back down in the chair and strapped me in.

"Where is he?" he snapped.

I felt a kind of fogginess in my head, and my thoughts became scattered and detached from reality. I wasn't sure where I was anymore and was far too confused to hear his questions. It sounded like someone was speaking to me underwater, and I just stared at him, lost and dazed. It didn't take long for me to lose consciousness all together.

When I came to, I wasn't back in my cell but was still in the lab. This time, I was back on the table, strapped down like a mental patient.

"You need to learn," one of the men snarled at me. "You keep lying to us."

I tried to move but was strapped down too tightly. "I already told you I wasn't lying."

"Which is also a lie," he spat.

He came toward me and dripped the same liquid on my forehead. This time it burned.

"Stop," I yelled. "Please! Take it off!"

"Shut up!" he shouted back at me.

I started yelling, almost screaming at him. It felt like acid was eating away at my skin. He wiped it away with a dry cloth, but I could still feel it scorching me.

"What the hell did you do to me?" I shouted.

Nobody answered me, and I started feeling like I did the first time I was in Keller's office. I wasn't sure where I was.

One of the men unstrapped me from the table and dragged me to the chair. I saw his eyes transform into the golden eyes of a cat. I tried to squeeze my eyes shut, telling myself it couldn't be real.

He reached toward me, and I saw he had claws. He pulled at my hair, ripping it out by the roots. I screamed, but he didn't stop. He began pulling at my limbs as if he were trying to tear me apart. I begged him to stop, begged him to just kill me.

"I won't hurt you if you stay calm," he said.

I couldn't stay calm. Not when he was clawing at my arms, leaving deep gashes on my flesh. Blood ran down the lengths of my limbs and dripped onto the floor. The cuts burned, but he kept slashing at me, kept ripping at the soft flesh on my arms, tearing me to shreds. I fought, and I screamed, but the assault did not cease. His claws were like those of a wild animal. I could feel pain entering my chest as it became difficult to breathe. He continued the attack, but I could feel myself slipping away. I could no longer even scream from the torture. Finally, the pain left me unconscious.

When I came to, I was still frantic, believing I was still in the lab. When I sat up, I saw that I was back in my cell. I examined my arms where the man had ripped apart my skin. I realized there were no bandages and no marks—no gashes, no cuts, not even any bruises save for the familiar finger marks on my upper arms. I had some ligature scars on my shins and around my torso but none of the torn flesh that I could swear was there only moments ago. I groaned and covered my face with my hands. More drugs. It had to be. None of it was real. More drugs, more hallucinations. When would it just end?

It must have been late because I had been asleep when she woke me up.

"Jane."

I flew up, gasping, bearing my teeth. I raised my fists instinctively, ready to defend myself. I lowered my hands when my eyes adjusted, and I saw it was a young girl, maybe a few years older than me with dirty blond hair and big, round green eyes.

"It's okay," she said. "It's me."

"Alex?"

I could see her nod her head even in the dark.

"How did you…?"

"I told you the locks are simplistic."

"They're going to see you."

"Yeah," she said. "So get up and come with me."

My energy immediately returned when I realized she must have been in a rush.

"That switch change you asked about…happens in about two minutes from what I know."

"How would you know?"

"I have made it a point to focus on when the lights go on and off and the sounds of footsteps that echo throughout the complex."

I pressed my fingers to my temples, nodding reflexively.

"Okay, so what's the plan?"

She chuckled quietly. "Run."

"That's it?" I hissed. "Run?"

"Run," she repeated, "fast!"

I didn't have time to gather my courage. I acted on instinct alone and relied on adrenalin to keep my feet moving. The concrete floors were cold on my bare feet, and the air was dead still. The door was opening as I raced toward it. Alex escaped first, but I pushed forward out the door. The guards came after us immediately, yelling and cursing, calling out orders to each other and requesting back up on their radios. I felt something strike the back of my head just as I ran past the threshold of the complex and into the grass outside. I stumbled forward but regained my balance and continued running. My vision blurred from the blow, and I reached my hands out in front of me to make sure I wouldn't run face-first into a wall. My skull was stinging and burning, and my heart thumped in my ears.

I saw Alex halt a few feet ahead and turn in my direction. She frantically signaled for me to hurry as the calls of the guards came louder. I strode up the grassy hill as fast as I could, glancing back at the complex, and I met up with Alex at an empty road. My heart plunged into my stomach. As long as there was nobody around, they would continue to follow us. We could see the tiny globes of flashlights behind us. I wasn't sure how much longer I could run, and my head was still throbbing.

"We have to keep going," Alex pressed. "We can't slow down."

"Alex, I have been in a cell for I don't even know how long. I have no energy!"

"Then find some," she snapped, grabbing my arm and practically dragging me with her down the road.

The street lamps on the corner clicked on, and relief flooded over me. I knew nobody would be following us into a well-lit area. We slowed our pace to a walk, and I listened to our heavy breathing.

"I don't recognize this road," I said, glancing at the trees and dense forests. There wasn't a house or building in sight.

"Neither do I," she answered. "Just keep walking, and something will look familiar."

I nodded, hoping she was right.

I could feel the knots in my hair and the dirt and blood still caked on my face. I was terrified of how I must look. I had lost at least six pounds and probably looked like a skeleton. Alex had more shape to her body than I did but still appeared just as sick and dirty. We couldn't risk anybody seeing us. We still had too much work to do before we could get Keller. Going to the police now could ruin everything.

The sky was beginning to light up a bit by the time we stopped. My legs and feet were aching. I sat beside Alex on the curb.

"Do you have a plan?" I asked.

She shook her head. "I hadn't planned past getting out of there."

I was about to rest my eyes when I spotted headlights coming our way. We both sprang up instantly, but we were too late. The car pulled up beside us, and the window slid down.

"Jane?"

I knew that voice and the word that never sounded quite like my name. I knew I should have been in shock, but it was almost like I had expected it. I was no more surprised that he found me than I had ever been.

"Aidan!"

"Get in!" he said.

I sat silently for a moment. My head was still stinging and burning.

"Are you okay?" It was the first thing he had said since he started driving.

I glanced over at him, and his face was blank. He was staring at the road. I turned to look at Alex, but she had her head down, seemingly ignoring everything.

"I'm fine," I said.

My memory flashed with all the torture I had endured and the image of Becky dead on the pavement, and my eyes filled with unshed tears.

"I don't know why I even asked you that," he said.

"What do you mean?"

"There is no way you are okay," he said, "either of you. What I meant to ask...is what the hell happened?"

I turned around to look at Alex again, and she finally looked up at me. Streaks of dirt on her face had been washed away by her tears.

"Jane?" he pressed.

"I...I don't know how to answer that."

"What did they do to you?"

I searched my mind for a response, but Alex interrupted.

"Everything," she said, sobbing. "They did everything."

Aidan didn't reply. He barely blinked, but I could see an obvious hardness on his face.

"We're okay," I told him. "Really. We got out."

"You got out?" he snapped. "Do you have any idea how long you have been gone?"

I shook my head. "A couple weeks maybe?"

He scoffed. "Really?" His features tensed again, and he swerved, pulling the car into park.

"Jane, if you don't want to talk about it, that's fine, but do not pretend you are okay. You have been gone for months."

"Months?"

"Yes!" he hissed. "Rudy is going crazy worrying about you, and I haven't been able to bring myself to look at your dad."

I covered my face with my hands. Through all the hell I had endured, I had forgotten about them.

"Okay, at least explain to me how the hell you got out of there."

"That was all Alex," I said, gesturing to her. "They hit me pretty hard in the back of my head, but we got close enough to well-lit areas, and they stayed back."

"They *will* come after you," he said. "You know that, right?"

I sighed and nodded. "Yeah."

"Okay, now that we know where the compound is, we can take care of Keller."

"Just like that?"

He smiled, and it almost surprised me. He glanced at me and chuckled quietly. "Have you forgotten who you're talking to?"

I felt a smile creep its way onto my face.

"Let's get you both cleaned up," he said. "You can shower, rest, and eat at Walter's. We'll deal with Becky and your dad tomorrow. Sound okay?"

My heart immediately plunged into my stomach when the image of Becky sprawled out on the concrete entered my mind. I tried to stay composed, but my eyes filled with tears.

"Aidan...Becky..."

I choked on my voice. Aidan turned to glance at me and seemed confused by my tears.

"Jane, what is it?" he asked. "Did I say something wrong?"

I was able to choke out two words between my sobs. "Becky's dead."

He glanced at me again and pulled his eyebrows together.

"What?"

"Keller!" I shouted. My sadness had shifted to anger. "The bastard killed her!"

"When?"

"Before he took me," I said. "He killed her then kidnapped me."

"Jane..."

I stopped, realizing that certain way he said my name.

"Jane," he said again, "Becky is alive."

I felt as if my heart had skipped a beat, and my entire body got shivers. "Wha—what?"

"She came to find me the next morning," he said. "She had an awful bruise on her face and a mild concussion but is otherwise fine."

"Oh my God. I have to see her, Aidan. I want to go see her now."

"No," he said. "No, Jane, we are going to Walter's first to get you cleaned up. Both of you. Nobody needs to see you like this."

I really had no room to argue. I hadn't even planned past getting out of the compound alive.

Aidan reached under his seat and pulled out a bottle of water.

"Here," he said, handing it to me. "There is a bottle of aspirin in the glove compartment."

"Thanks," I muttered.

I downed two tablets then passed the water to Alex.

She barely looked at me, and neither Aidan or I could get her to talk to us at all. We wanted to get her back to her family, but she was locked inside her own head, completely unresponsive.

It was all sort of a blur. There was a lot of crying and hugging, but my mind was too foggy to focus. I barely heard Becky's remarks or Ethan's questions. I heard Aidan telling them that everything was okay like he always did.

Becky helped me up the stairs and into the bathroom. Even after the meal at Walter's, the knotting in my stomach was getting worse, and I was already out of breath. Everything ached.

"What the hell happened to you?" Becky whispered.

"It's a long story," I answered.

"We were supposed to be in this together," she said. I could hear her voice breaking. "I was supposed to be there to make sure this didn't happen."

"Becky, this wasn't your fault," I said. "I thought you were dead when Keller left you like that."

"I didn't even wake up until the morning. I went straight to Aidan when I realized you had disappeared."

I pressed my fingers to my temples, unable to continue the conversation as the throbbing in my head returned.

"Here," Becky said. "I'll give you some privacy. After you get cleaned up, we will have something ready for you to eat."

I nodded. "Thank you."

The shower felt normal, and for fleeting moments, I felt at home again where things were as ordinary as things had ever been for me. My body ached, but the heat relaxed the soreness in my muscles, and I imagined that the water was cleansing me of all the horrors of the past months. I was not able to forget that we still had to deal with getting Alex back to her family, but she still was not talking. I wondered then how much more trauma she must have suffered to shut down the way she had. It was so unfair that people had to be terrorized by monsters like Keller. Maybe I had to be involved to stop it. Even if I couldn't stop it from happening to me, I could stop it from happening to others. Maybe that was my whole purpose in life. It was nice to think I had a purpose, that my life was something more than one insane struggle after another. With life, you never could be sure.

I tried talking to Alex for a while. She wasn't engaging, but sometimes she would glance up at me or smile. At least it was progress.

"Aidan is a good guy," I said. "Without him, I would not have survived any of the things I have been through."

I left out the fact that I would never have experienced them either. I was trying to make her feel better, not frighten her more.

"Alex…we want to help you," I pleaded. "Please. Tell me something —a name, an address—anything."

She looked away as if she was shutting down again. I grabbed a notepad and a pen off my desk and handed it to her.

"Here," I said. "Can you write?"

She looked at the paper for a moment, then back at me.

She picked up the pen and jotted something down. When she handed the notebook back, she had turned away from me.

I can't go home.

That's all she had written. I wasn't going to get any more out of her yet. I needed to let her come around on her own.

I needed to get away—to get away from the looks and the questions and the way Ethan always wanted to say something but swallowed his words and shifted his weight, trying to mask his discomfort. Alex had slept on the couch the night before and still was not speaking. I couldn't stay a moment longer but knew I couldn't leave Alex here by herself with Ethan, so I convinced Becky to spend some time with her in my room and try watching some movies for a little while so I could clear my head.

Time with Aidan seemed like it was long overdue.

"I want to take you somewhere," he said. "I feel like it's time."

I nodded. "Okay."

We got in the car, and my nerves immediately went into overdrive, and I found myself wringing my hands together and sighing heavily.

"You okay?" Aidan asked without taking his eyes off the road.

"Um…yeah," I answered. "Yeah, I'm just feeling a bit anxious for some reason."

"Don't worry," he said. "This will be good for you. It will make you feel better."

I couldn't respond. I just watched the mist in the air, not quite rain, and imagined things were normal. It didn't take long for me to recognize the stretch of road lined with trees and the exact place he parked the car.

"Aidan, I don't think…" I couldn't finish my sentence.

"Jane, I want you to see that you're safe. I want to show you that the clearing is nothing more than that."

I shook my head. "I don't know."

He touched my hand. "It's okay. I promise."

I pulled my eyebrows together and nodded reluctantly. My movements were slowed as if I were trying to put off actually walking into the woods—the place of my horrors. I followed Aidan and grabbed his hand when we stepped into the circle of cleared land. The stones had not been moved, and nothing seemed different than before. I was terrified that Dorian would come stepping out from behind the trees at any moment. Even as my memory replayed the day I had shot him to death, the fear did not relent. Aidan leaned against a tree and pulled me into his chest, wrapping his arms around my waist. His embrace warmed me, and I suddenly felt very relaxed.

Something about the clearing seemed surreal, like I wasn't really there at all.

"Are you okay?" he asked me.

I nodded. "It's strange being back here," I said, "like this."

"I know. I want you to feel safe again, Jane. This was the best way I knew how."

I smiled. "Thank you." I sighed, trying to savor being close to him again. Something about it didn't feel quite real. I felt detached in some way and realized in that moment that I had felt that way since we first escaped the compound. Time seemed to move more quickly, and sometimes things didn't connect in sensible ways in my head.

I suddenly felt dizzy and moved away from Aidan to get my thoughts together. I tried to shake off the uncomfortable feelings when movement caught my eye. I instinctively turned to the direction of the stones and saw what had captured my attention. I instantly choked on my breath, and my entire body felt paralyzed. It was a man cloaked in black, staring directly at me. He was still but focused, and he wasn't alone. From every corner of the forest, more of them were appearing—all of them in long, black coverings like something from a nightmare, and they were all bearing daggers. I turned to Aidan, but he was just standing there with no expression and no reaction.

"Aidan?"

I backed away as they came forward.

"Aidan!"

He was still not moving even as I began screaming his name and stumbling over my feet as the men advanced, desperately trying to get to me. I turned and ran, tripping over fallen branches and sticks. I ignored the cuts and stabs of the brush as I rushed through the forest. I had no conception anymore of where I was or how far I had gone, but I didn't stop. I ran until my feet ached and my muscles burned. I could feel myself running out of steam as my knees gave out, and I fell face-first into the mud. I rolled over onto my back, panting and struggling to catch my breath. I couldn't see or hear anyone coming toward me, but I was also very lost in the deep part of the woods. It would be dark soon, and I was all alone.

All I could think about was the blank look on Aidan's face, thinking he must have planned this—all of it. Maybe The Sevren were never gone at all. Maybe this was all an elaborate part of Aidan's plan. But that didn't make sense either. So much was going through my mind. I was beginning to feel tired, and my head was hurting again. I closed my eyes and immediately felt a cloudy feeling pulling me out of my current state and ripping me violently out of the cold woods and into the blinding light of a ceiling lamp. I was sure I was dreaming but somehow felt very present, and all of the past events, from escaping the compound to being in the woods with Aidan, faded into a vague and surreal past.

"Miss?" I heard.

My body stiffened when I recognized the voice. I turned my head in his direction, and before I made the choice to, I heard myself scream as the man in the lab coat lifted a syringe.

Chapter Sixteen

"IT'S JUST A PAIN KILLER," I heard him say. "Just relax. You have a concussion."

I could feel a kind of relief slither into the ache in my head. I tried to open my eyes and force myself awake. I realized then that this was no dream. I never escaped the compound with Alex. None of it had really happened. I still had no idea where Aidan was, and Becky was still dead. Everything came flooding back to me, and I knew—I was never getting out.

I remembered the guard smashing me over the head with what I had believed to be a flashlight. I must have been knocked unconscious and dragged back to the lab. What about Alex?

Oh God. I hope she made it out!

I was having a hard time being sure of where reality had stopped and the dream had begun. Did I even make it to the door of the complex as I thought? Perhaps the head injury was from something else. Maybe Alex and I had never even gotten out of our cells at all. I winced as the painful pressure behind my eyes returned.

"Roger, you can take her back," I heard.

The man helped me off the table and led me back to my cell. There was a bowl of food on the floor—the same gray mush they always tried to feed me. I was then wishing that at least the meal at Walter's had been real. I tapped on the wall and did not hear a reply.

"Alex?"

No answer. I sighed and rested my forehead against the wall. She must have made it out. At the same time that made me happy, I was not looking forward to being all alone again. There was a fear in the back of my mind that Keller may have killed her or that one of the guards had hit her a bit harder than he hit me. I tried to push the thoughts away and believe she escaped. She must have escaped; I refused to let myself believe otherwise.

Tony yanked me out of my cell either very late or very early the next day. He pulled me down the hallway. There was no light peeking in from the little windows, so it must have been dark. He led me back to those metal stairs, and panic crept into my chest. There was no point in putting up a fight, so I climbed the stairs. He took me back to the bathroom with the shower stalls. This time there were towels on the counter, along with another set of clothing.

"Ten minutes," he snarled.

"Or you come in to get me," I said. "I know."

My hair was a matted mess, and my skin was dull and lifeless. I moved as quickly as I could before Tony could come in. As soon as I was dressed and came back outside, he cuffed me and signaled me to follow him back down the stairs. I obeyed. He led me down the hallway on the lower floor and practically threw me into Keller's office and shut the door.

"Ah," Keller sneered, smiling like we were friends.

"Why am I here?"

His smile returned, and I could tell he was suppressing laughter. "You didn't think I would let you run away, did you?"

"I didn't run away."

"Just because you didn't succeed doesn't make the deed any less of an offense."

I stiffened, realizing I had nothing to say in my defense. He was not going to listen to any pleas, protest, or apologies anyway. I figured I would just have to take the punishment he had planned and hope for the best. Maybe he would just kill me after all. That may be better than the alternative. I waited, hoping he may just stick me with a needle and take me back to my cell. He didn't.

"Stand up," he said.

"What?"

"Now—on your feet."

I sighed and stood up. I could feel the handcuffs cutting into my wrists.

"Can't you take the cuffs off?"

He laughed but didn't say a word. He reached for something under his desk and revealed what looked like a metal pipe. I cringed, knowing this was going to be bad. He approached me and lifted the weapon. I shut my eyes and prepared myself for the bash to the head.

To my surprise, I felt a terrible pain in my leg, and I collapsed to the floor, heaving and sobbing. He hit me again in the back as I lay hunched over on the floor, coughing. I was gasping for breath as the agony forced more coughs and cries from my chest. Before I could feel his last blow, I passed out, still feeling the horrible throbbing in my body.

When I awoke, the pain had not ceased, but there was an obvious coolness from a pain killer. My leg was wrapped in a splint, and I could see that it was all shades of black and purple. There was clearly no way of running now. I concentrated on not moving my leg or even flexing the muscles in hopes that it would prevent it from hurting any more. I drank the water set on the floor and choked down some of the gray mush. I was feeling sick and fatigued, so much that the dizziness would attack me even as I was lying down, not moving. I was still losing weight, and my muscles were getting weaker and weaker. I truly felt myself diminishing —dying.

There was almost no point in fighting if only for it to end quickly. I wished only for the torture to stop. There was a strange comfort in the soreness I was feeling. As long as I could still feel pain, I felt that Keller had not yet broken me. I still had my humanity. The hours passed, and the stiffness and throbbing in my leg had begun to fade into the background. I didn't even attempt to get out of bed. I knew one of Keller's men would eventually drag me back to the lab anyway.

I was so alone. Alex was gone, and all I ever heard were the muffled voices and the creaking of footsteps on the upstairs floors of the complex. I was going mad with loneliness. At times, I even wished to see Keller so I could scream at him—anything to end the silence. When the lights went out that night, I tried to sleep. I had no conception if it was even night time. The lights turned on and off at odd, uneven intervals. I was sure it was a way to confuse me. I slept deeply, finally able to ignore the soreness, and found myself awakened by the strange, yet familiar smell—of smoke.

I opened my eyes to see that I was not alone. There was a man standing before me. He was young and nicely dressed, but I didn't recognize him. I threw my hands up defensively.

"It's okay," he said. "I'm here to help you."

"Help me?"

He nodded, but I kept my hands in front of my chest. My leg was broken, and there was no way I could fight, so why was he lying?

"You need to get up," he snapped. "The compound is on fire."

The dizziness attacked me again as the smell of smoke became more potent, and I could see that the air was beginning to get cloudy. Whether this man could be trusted or not, I could not stay here when the place was going up in flames.

I stumbled to my feet, but he began leading me down the hallway, opposite of the door. I hobbled along on my one leg, lagging behind.

"Where are you taking me?" I snapped.

"Trust me," he said. "Just don't argue."

"I don't understand what's going on."

"Do you know anyone by the name of Morgan?"

I was taken off guard. I recognized the name immediately, and memories began to deluge over me. Voices from past summers assaulted my ears, and I knew what was happening. He was here. Aidan was here. He had been planning to get me out the whole time. We continued down the hall, and the adrenaline rushing through my veins was enough for me to keep up even with the pain searing through my leg. I clutched the man's arm as he rushed through the smoke that was now chasing us through the compound. We stopped just feet from a set of cement steps leading down to another, lower floor, one I had no idea even existed.

"Come on," he said.

"What?" I yelled. "No. I am not going to let you lock me up in here to burn. Tell me where Aidan is."

"Jane, trust me," he said. "This *is* where he is."

I wasn't even thinking about budging when I heard a familiar voice call my name.

"Jane? Is that you?"

"Alex?"

The sound of her voice brought that adrenaline back into me, and I practically fell over my feet to get to the bottom of the stairs. She was as young as she sounded, with almost dirty blond hair and big, familiar, green eyes. I must have been knocked out when we made it to the door. She was just as dirty and thin as me. She was in a cell, and there were at least five other cells with other prisoners. The man unlocked her door, and I ran in and hugged her.

"Oh, Jane," she said with a whimper. "Your leg."

"Yeah. My punishment for running."

She opened her mouth to speak but was interrupted.

"Jane!"

I turned immediately, knowing it was Aidan, and fell into his arms. Feeling that familiar closeness almost brought tears to my eyes. I knew those arms; I knew the hardness of his chest and the build of his shoulders. I knew this as something that was a part of me, and I couldn't let go.

"Jane, we have to go," he said. "Now."

"You're crazy," I said.

He smiled that beautiful smile. "I know, but I couldn't let you stay here, so I got some friends together, and we conspired to take down Keller."

"And now?"

"Now we have to run," he said. "The place is on fire."

He lifted me into his arms, and I whimpered from the pain in my body but didn't complain. He carried me through the hallways, and I could feel the heat from the approaching blaze. He headed toward a doorway but was thrown back by a burst of flames. My arm was burning. I glanced at it, noticing the sleeve of my polyester shirt was on fire. Aidan quickly doused the smoldering fabric with the end of his shirt. The pain was intense, but I tried to ignore. There were the awful sounds of coughing and gagging followed by the fumbling of feet as we all struggled to find a way out. We turned another corner, and the blaze came rapidly toward us. Aidan ran, clutching me tighter in his arms. He leapt over the fire that was licking at the floor. I could hear the stomping and heavy breaths of the others behind us. I felt Aidan stiffen, and I buried my face in his chest.

I felt a draft of cold air soothing my wounded arm, but Aidan had not stopped running. I looked up to notice we were running through a thick wood. I could see the compound behind us, completely engulfed in flames.

Our surroundings became covered by shadow as we emerged into the deeper parts of the forest. Aidan's pace slowed, and the others arrived at his side, still coughing and heaving. My own lungs were still burning, and I had not even been running. The smoke and ash assaulted us even through the thickness of the trees.

"Are you okay?" Aidan whispered.

I nodded but wasn't able to respond. I was alive but pretty far from okay. Nobody said anything as the night became darker. I could feel Aidan's heart pounding and his arms getting weaker.

"You can put me down," I said. "Rest."

He shook his head. "Not yet. We need to be much farther away before we stop."

"I think she's right," Alex said. "Carrying her any farther is only going to wear you out more."

"It's not like she weighs a thing," he said with a teasing tone behind his words.

"We have nice coverage here," a male voice chimed in. "We should rest for a little while."

Aidan nodded. "All right, but we can't stay long. We need to keep moving as quickly as possible."

"Where's the car?" the same man asked.

"I have my phone in my pocket. I should get a text as soon as she's where I told her to meet us," Aidan answered.

"Who is meeting us?" I asked.

He smiled. "Luna, of course."

I felt a sense of happiness at the sound of her name. I had missed her more than I realized. That was when the pain and guilt of losing Becky came flooding back to me, and I found myself crying, unable to stop it. Aidan didn't even ask me what was wrong; he just held me close until I was able to calm down. I knew what happened to her was because of me. Aidan told me not to get her involved, and I ignored him simply because I was being my stupid, stubborn self. I sighed, wiping my eyes with the back of my hand.

"It's okay to cry," Aidan said. It was like he knew exactly what I was thinking. "You have been through a lot. I'll make sure you get through this."

I nodded, unable to say anything. I couldn't say it out loud. It was too horrible, too painful. What Keller had put me through paled in comparison to what I would do to myself if I couldn't forgive myself…and I couldn't—at least not yet.

Aidan sat on the ground behind me and pulled me into his chest. I fell limp against him and relaxed. I could feel myself already dozing off. It was the first time I had felt even a small sense of safety. That's when the joy of getting out finally set in. It was over. We were free.

"Alex," I said. "We did it."

I heard her laugh. "We did," she said. "Ah. Finally!"

"Thanks to all of you," I added. "I can't tell you how much it means to me."

"We didn't have a choice," a girl said. She was a little older than me but still had a youthful look to her. "We couldn't let Keller keep torturing people."

I nodded. "What happened to him?"

"No," Aidan said. "We are not going to talk about any of that yet. He can't hurt you anymore, Jane. That is all you need to know."

I sighed, realizing he was right. I didn't want to talk about it. Knowing Keller had no control over me was all I needed to know then. When things settled, I knew Aidan would tell me everything. That was just the way he worked.

I must have fallen asleep because Aidan woke me up, telling me we had to go meet Luna. He picked me up and carried me through the woods, following the tiny ray from a flashlight. We reached the edge of the woods and stepped onto an empty road.

"Where's Luna?" I asked.

"Around the corner," he answered. "Don't worry."

We walked for a few long minutes. My eyes were still heavy, but the pain killers were wearing off, and I was aching too much to fall back asleep. I tried to ignore the pain and not make things any more stressful for Aidan. I knew the way I looked must have terrified him. I recognized Aidan's red Mustang the second I saw it. He picked up his pace toward the car. There was a silver Toyota parked behind Luna.

"Walter," he said. "You and I are going with Luna. The others are going with him."

I nodded.

"Jane?" Alex said, walking up beside Aidan. "I will see you again. Maybe when all of this is over, we can be friends."

I smiled. "I would like that."

She mirrored my smile and got into Walter's car.

Aidan set me carefully in the back of Luna's car and got in the passenger's seat.

"Jane," Luna sang like she always did, "how are you feeling?"

Aidan interrupted before I could answer. "She's hurt," he said. "She needs some help before her father sees her like this."

"No," I protested. "I just want to see Ethan. He's a doctor, remember?"

Luna looked to Aidan for his answer.

"No," he said. "Jane, we will take you to Ethan, but you don't want him to see you like this. Just let Luna clean you up and bandage up your leg a little better. Ethan can do the rest. I promise."

"Do I really look that awful?"

He opened his mouth to speak, but I interrupted him. "Don't answer that."

Luna started the car.

"There's some aspirin in the glove compartment," she said to Aidan, "and some water in the back seat."

I grabbed the water bottle out of the bag on the seat beside me, and Aidan handed me the aspirin.

"This will have to do until we can get you to Luna's."

"What happened to you?" Luna asked.

I shook my head. "I just can't talk about it. Just not yet."

"I'm sorry," she said. "I didn't mean to pry."

"You weren't," I said. "I promise to tell you both everything when I'm ready."

The rest of the drive was silent. I paid no attention to the direction we were headed. I didn't care to know where the compound was, sure that I would never be able to forget otherwise and every street would remind me how close or far I was from it. It wasn't until we reached Luna's house that I recognized where we were.

Aidan helped me out of the car then carried me to the house.

"What time is it?" I asked.

Aidan glanced at his watch. "Two-thirty."

I shook my head. "I never even knew if it was day or night the entire time I was in there."

"I know," he said, stepping into the house and setting me on the couch. "It was Keller's way of confusing you. The longer you were in there, the easier it would be for him to break you."

"I was giving in, Aidan," I said. "I just wanted it to end."

"You wouldn't have," he said. "I know you, Jane. You would have kept fighting. You survived more than many others."

"He tormented me. Kept me in there for… God, I don't even know how long."

"You have been gone a total of eight days."

"Eight days?" I yelled. "No. That can't be right."

"Jane relax," he coaxed. "I know it feels like a lot longer—"

"Months, Aidan," I cried. "It feels like several months."

He sighed. "But it hasn't been. You're okay."

I shook my head. "I can't believe I could have been *that* disoriented."

"It was all part of Keller's plan."

Luna emerged from the kitchen with a first aid kit.

"Chicken is in the oven," she said. "I will fix you up and get a hot meal in you before we take you home."

I nodded. "Thank you."

She helped me into the bath. I kept my burned arm out of the water. Luna had put some herbal burn cream on it, which seemed to help. My hair was so matted that it took a ton of conditioner to even pull a brush through it. Luna ended up trimming off a good five inches. After I was clean and dressed, she started with my leg, taking off the splint and lightly rubbing some type of cream over it. The lightest touch had me wincing.

"This will help with the swelling," she said.

She bound it tightly in a medical wrap before attaching a higher quality splint.

She opened the case again and pulled out a syringe. My memory flashed with every single time I had been stuck with one of those, and I immediately started to panic. I pulled myself farther up on the couch and started flailing my arms.

"Jane, it's okay," she said, but I only heard Keller's voice—his lies and his taunts. I took a quick swing, knocking her to the floor.

Aidan pinned my arms to my sides. I continued to struggle until I saw that Luna no longer had the needle in her hand.

She stood up and placed a hand over her now reddened cheek. I realized I had hit her. Shame washed over me, and my eyes filled with hot tears.

"Oh my God, Luna. I'm so sorry."

"Jane, it's okay," she said. "If you don't want the shot, it's okay."

"No, it's not that," I said. "It's just…"

"He drugged you, didn't he?" Aidan asked.

The tears spilled over, and I nodded.

He enfolded me in his arms. "Oh God," he murmured.

"It will help with the pain," she said. "But you don't have to take it."

"It's okay," I said, moving away from Aidan. "I can handle it."

"Are you sure?"

I nodded. "I'm so sorry. I didn't mean to—"

"It's okay," she interrupted. "You've been through hell. I'm not upset with you."

"I'm ready."

She nodded and pressed the needle into my arm. I tried to push away the visions of the compound. I kept my eyes on Aidan, reminding myself where I was until Luna was finished.

"Let me see your arm," she said.

I pulled up the sleeve of my shirt.

"Take it off," she said.

"What?"

"Jane, just take the shirt off."

Aidan laughed. "I'll leave," he said. "I'll go check on the chicken."

"Okay, good," she said. She examined my chest and stomach. "It's just your arm. You do have a couple of broken ribs, so I need to wrap you up."

She spread some kind of burn cream over my arm again and put another medical wrap around my torso. I put my shirt back on, and Aidan returned with two mugs.

"Here," he said. "Drink this."

"More herbal tea?" I smiled.

Luna smiled back. "My specialty," she said. "Thanks, James."

Aidan gave me a few pieces of French bread to eat before dinner along with the tea. The tonic was as sweet as I remembered, and I felt a kind of heaviness come over me.

"Sleep," Aidan said. "I will wake you up when dinner is ready."

I nodded, feeling the cramping in my stomach at the thought. I fell asleep quickly, comfortable as I had always been on Luna's couch.

When Aidan woke me for dinner, it felt like I had been asleep for days. It had been a long time since I had slept so soundly. The meal was

Luna's typical amazing cooking. I ate slowly, trying to savor every bite that wasn't tasteless, gray mush. I ate until my stomach hurt and couldn't eat more. It was well past four in the morning, so I knew I had to wait to go home.

"Tomorrow?" I asked Aidan, getting up from the table.

"Yes," he said. "I will take you home first thing tomorrow after you get some more sleep."

"Is this real?"

He pulled his eyebrows together. "Is what real?"

"This," I answered. "This—you, Luna, the escape. All of it?"

He smiled. "It is. I know you must have dreamed of it every night."

I shook my head. "We tried to escape. Alex and I. We tried to escape, and as I made it to the door, I was hit over the head with a flashlight. I had this vivid dream of getting out and being home with Ethan and you…even Becky. I woke up back in the lab."

He pulled me into his chest. "This time, you are really out," he said. "It's over."

I started crying again at the thought of never being able to talk through it with Becky. She always knew what to say. There was never a time when a conversation with her didn't help in some way. Aidan hushed me and told me everything was okay. It only made me more upset.

"Please stop telling me that," I murmured.

"It's true," he said. "I promise."

I moved away from him, and I flopped back down on the couch.

"It's not okay," I said, weeping. "It will never be okay."

He sat beside me. "It'll take time."

I shook my head. "Don't you understand that what happened to Becky is my fault?"

He shook his head and moved his eyes to the ground. "Becky… I…it wasn't your fault, Jane."

I just shook my head again. "I brought her with me, Aidan, even after you asked me not to."

"She would have come no matter what. You and I both know that."

"That doesn't change the fact that I basically killed my sister."

He sighed. "Well, you don't need to be so dramatic, Jane. Just call her. She's not even mad at you."

"Wh—what?"

I thought for a minute that he was joking with me and had the intense desire to pummel him for it, but the look on his face told me otherwise.

"Just call her."

"How...? I don't understand."

"I don't think we are on the same page here," he said with a chuckle.

"I thought...Becky..." I paused, and my head began to ache. I pressed my fingers to my temples. "Aidan, I thought she was dead."

"What?" He almost shouted the word. "Oh, Jane. Oh my God. I am so sorry. I should have said something. Becky is fine. She was complaining of a terrible headache for a couple days and had a nasty head laceration. It bled a lot, but she was okay. I am pretty sure she just had a concussion. Luna gave her some pain killers, and she's been fine since then. Even tried insisting on coming with me to get you out."

I wasn't sure at first how I felt. I was confused. When it sank in, joy filled me like I never thought it could, and I found myself in tears again. Becky was alive the entire time. It seemed then like nothing could get better. I wanted to focus on her, but I had one question that couldn't wait. "What became of Keller?"

"He isn't dead," Aidan answered. "We have him though. He can't hurt you anymore."

"What do you mean *we*?"

He laughed. "Well, not us," he said, waving his hands, "but old members of The Silver Wing have him in custody. He has answers we need before we...well, you know."

"We can't kill him," I said. "We have to take him to Detective Styles. I want the entire world to know what happened to Danny!"

"Jane, Danny's death has been avenged. That's what matters."

"That's not good enough!" I shouted. "I want him to confess what he did. Death is too easy for him, Aidan. I want him to suffer. I want him to be locked away in a cage like the animal he is."

He put his hands up in defense. "Okay," he said calmly. "Okay, you're right. You should get a say in this after everything that's

155

happened, but I think it's best to wait a few days. Talk to Becky and Ethan, and then decide if you still feel that way."

I nodded. "Fine, but I am calling Becky now."

"It's four in the morning, Jane."

I put out my hand. "I don't care."

He sighed and handed me his silver cell phone. Becky's cell number was in his contacts. It barely got through one ring before she answered.

"Aidan!" she yelled. "What's wrong?"

"Becky?" I tried to say. I was already in tears just from the sound of her voice.

"Oh my God, Jane! Are you okay? Where are you?"

"I'm okay," I said. "I'm at Luna's. Aidan promised to take me home tomorrow."

"Good," she said. "He can take me with you because I'm coming over."

I laughed. "It's okay. You don't have to do that."

"Oh, whatever," she said with a laugh. "You and I both know that isn't true."

I already heard her car door slamming. "Okay, okay," I said.

"Be there in ten."

"Becky, it's a twenty-minute drive."

"Yeah, when you drive like Jane," she said. "I will see you in ten."

Becky got to Luna's in about fifteen minutes and apologized for being late when I opened up. I hugged her so tightly she was the one complaining.

"Ow," she groaned. "Jane, I can't breathe."

Aidan laughed. "Does it to me all the time."

I smiled but couldn't hide my tears.

"Don't cry," she said and hugged me again. "You can crush me. It's okay."

"I thought you were dead."

She pulled away from me. "What?" she yelled. "Why would you think that?"

"When Keller slammed you against the wall," I started, "you weren't moving. You were bleeding. I thought…"

"Well, he didn't," she said. "Gave me one wicked migraine but I'm fine now."

I nodded.

"You on the other hand," she started and sat down on the couch signally me to follow. "Are *you* okay?"

"I'm fine."

"Good. Now I will ask you again. Are you okay?"

I sighed. "No. Not really."

"That's better. Now talk to me."

Chapter Seventeen

"DID you ever find out who Alex was?" I asked. "She didn't tell me much."

"Oh, Alex was a friend of mine," he answered. "Well, a friend of Ian's really."

"Wait. What?" I mused. "So…she was never a prisoner?"

"Well, she was," he answered, "but it was all a set up."

"That doesn't make sense."

"Don't get me wrong," he said. "She went through hell, which wasn't exactly part of the plan, but she knew we were going to get you two out. She was just waiting. When we didn't show up, she decided to try and escape herself. Apparently, it didn't work out."

"She was in there before I was."

"Well, yes," he said. "We knew about the compound very shortly after your meeting with Keller. Ian and his people have been trying to infiltrate for a while. We only found out Ian's plan when you went missing."

"So she's a Silver Wing?"

He shrugged. "Sort of."

"Sort of?"

"She's Ian's girlfriend," he said. "I guess that makes her guilty by association."

"So she knew who I was the entire time?"

He grimaced. "Pretty much."

"I really wish you would stop keeping things like that from me."

"The only reason I don't tell you things is because it's easier," he said. "If you knew that I was coming for you, things could have gone wrong. You may have slipped up and said something when Keller drugged you."

I nodded. "Well, I did say something about Luna when I thought Keller was you."

"You thought he was me?"

I laughed. "For a few minutes."

"What the hell did he give you?"

"I actually don't know," I answered. "I can't remember what he called it, but it was definitely some heavy duty, dangerous stuff."

"Did it hurt?"

I shook my head. "Only once when I literally thought he was tearing through my chest."

He grunted, and a sick look flickered across his face.

"Sorry," I mused. "It wasn't so bad."

"It's okay," he said. "You don't have to pretend. I know it was hell for you, Jane. I can handle it."

"You always feel awful when I tell you what I've been through."

"Well, of course I do, but I can handle it. I want to know. I want to be there for you."

"Then what do I tell the people who can't handle it?" I asked. "Like Ethan."

"Your father can handle more than you give him credit for," he said. "But just leave out the parts that you know will keep him up at night."

"Those are the parts that keep *me* up at night."

"If there is anything you are not ready to talk about, it's okay," he said, "but if you are ready, I would like to hear about what happened."

"I'm ready," I said.

I actually told him everything I could remember. Even when he seemed like he was going to be sick, I didn't stop. There were tears and painful flashbacks, but I continued through them. When I was finished, I wasn't sure what he was thinking.

"I'm sorry," was all he said.

I shook my head. "It's not your fault."

"I just wish I could have prevented this. You didn't want to meet with Keller, but I convinced you that it would be okay."

"It was the only way," I said. "You and I both know that."

He nodded and shrugged. "Still."

"What now?" I asked.

"Now?" he repeated. "Now, we go to see Ethan. Luna washed some clothes for you. I'm taking you home."

I wanted to see Ethan more than anything but was terrified of facing him at the same time. I had already put him through so much. I got dressed quickly, noticing that Luna's jeans were at least three inches too long for me, and her shirt was too loose in the top. It didn't bother me. I was thankful to be taken care of. My leg was still hurting, but the pain killers Luna had given me were helping immensely. I would have to let Ethan take a closer look at it to make sure I didn't need surgery and get a cast in place.

I daydreamed through the ride there, trying to keep myself calm. When we got there is when I suddenly realized how much I missed Ethan and my home. Aidan helped me to the front door.

"Should I knock?"

He nodded. "Walking in might not be the best option in these circumstances."

I knocked on the door, and my dad opened up in less than ten seconds. I could see that he had been crying, possibly for hours.

"Jane?"

"It's me, Dad. I'm all right."

He immediately broke into hysterics and pulled me into a hug. He didn't squeeze me half to death the way he usually did. His hug was weak, and I could feel his arms shaking from his sobs. I didn't try to say any consoling words; I just hugged him back, waiting for him to get ahold of himself.

He moved away from me but kept his hands on my shoulders. "What happened?" he asked. "Where have you been?"

He glanced down and noticed the crutches I had taken from Luna's. A sickened look came over his features.

"Dad, I'm okay," I said. "I promise."

"Have you been to the hospital yet?"

I shook my head. "I'm fine."

He put his hand on my back and led me into the living room to sit on the couch. "I'll be the judge of that," he said.

Aidan followed us inside and sat at the end of the couch.

"You need to tell him," Aidan said.

I nodded. "I know."

"Tell me what?" Ethan mused. "What happened to you?"

I sighed and started from the beginning. He didn't seem surprised, but the look on his face told me he was terrified. I tried to explain that Keller had been stopped and that I would be safe now. The Sevren is gone, Keller is in custody, and Aidan's friends are always watching for any signs of danger. We would all be safe now.

"Maybe you should go back to Florida," he said, "where you were before."

I shook my head. "Dad, really, everything is okay here now. I don't want to leave. North Bend is my home now."

He sighed and nodded. "Let me take a look at your leg. You may need a cast. You really should be in a hospital. Do you know what lack of food does to your organs?"

"I'm okay," I insisted even though I knew it wasn't true.

I winced as he lifted my leg, checking for anything more serious than a break. He was pretty upset even before knowing about my broken ribs or noticing my bandaged arm. I didn't know what to do to make things easier on him. I decided just to let him take care of me. That seemed like the only thing that could make him feel better.

"Who did this to you?" he murmured as he removed the splint from my leg to get a closer look. "Was it him, that Keller man?"

I nodded. "He had to punish me for trying to run away."

He shook his head. "Did he do…anything else?"

162

I pulled my eyebrows together. "What do you mean?"

He sighed and glanced at Aidan. "Just…anything…worse. Did he hurt you in other ways?"

Aidan understood first and looked to me. "She didn't mention it to me," he said. "Jane?"

I realized what they were talking about, and it suddenly seemed like what had happened to me wasn't as bad as it could have been.

"No," I said. "Keller may have stuck me with a few needles and broken my leg, but he never…touched me like that. Nobody did."

"Well, thank God for that," Ethan answered, putting the splint back on. "It's just a break. Nothing too serious. There's no infection, but you will need a cast."

"Okay."

"Try not to move your leg," he said. "I can put the cast on myself, but we need to get to the hospital. Is there anything else that's wrong?"

I shook my head.

"No head injuries?"

"Not that I know of," I said. "I was smacked with a flashlight, but that probably healed up. It doesn't hurt anymore."

He nodded. "Okay. I'll check it out when we get there just to be sure."

Aidan rode with us to the hospital, but we were all mostly silent the entire drive. I guess there was just nothing left to say. All I could do now was focus on getting better physically and mentally. I knew there were still a few more things I needed to do to get there.

I needed to see him. It didn't matter what I needed to say or what I might do. I just had to see him.

"I don't know why you must insist on this," she whispered. "What good will it do?"

"Becky, I don't expect you to understand," I answered. "I don't know myself why I have to do this. I don't have a choice."

She shook her head. "I'm coming with you."

I almost laughed. "Um…no, Becky. Not this time."

"Oh, please, Jane. I came with you before."

"Yeah, and you almost got yourself killed."

"Exactly," she answered. "And I am not dead, am I? He can't hurt either of us now, so what reason is there for me to *not* come?"

"You aren't going to let me argue with you on this, are you?"

"Oh, you can argue all you want, but I'm coming regardless."

I smiled. "Fine. But listen to Aidan if he tells you to stay back or something, okay?"

"Sure, sure."

Aidan led us down the steps of Ian's house to the basement where, apparently, they had built some sort of cage. It was very cliché. Seeing him there caged up like an animal with his face bruised and bloodied made me feel almost foolish for ever being afraid of him. He looked so pitiful and powerless.

"How does it feel?" I snarled. "Being kept in a cell?"

He didn't answer, but he looked up at me.

"You really thought you could win, didn't you? I told you it wouldn't work. It feels good to say 'I told you so.'"

He stood up and stepped closer to the rails to stare into my eyes. I didn't even back away. He couldn't hurt me now.

"You think you're so tough?" I teased. "Scary? Well, you aren't. You're nothing but a coward in a cage."

He lunged forward, reaching through the railings, clawing at me. I jumped back a few inches, and Aidan raised his pistol.

"I will shoot you if I have to," he threatened. Aidan hated guns, but I knew he meant it.

Keller settled back a few inches away. I stepped closer and used the last bit of anger I had left and spit in his face. He lunged again, but I had already turned my back and moved closer to the stairs.

Becky was there, waiting for me. I smiled at her, and she returned the grin, glancing back at Keller and shaking her head. "Pitiful," she murmured just loud enough for him to hear.

He snarled but still said nothing.

When we got back to the car, I felt the closure I was hoping it would bring me. The images would still haunt me, maybe for the rest of my life, but seeing him like that finally made me feel safe again.

"Thank you," I said.

"Of course," Aidan answered.

"So what now?"

"What do you mean?"

"What happens to him now?"

"Well, Ian beat him up pretty badly, and he confessed to where his headquarters are. We're sure his men are hiding out there."

"And?"

"And we need to stop them."

I sighed. "More fighting, Aidan?"

"No," he said. "Actually, I am not involved. This is Ian's mission, and he was sure to let me know it."

I laughed. "Good. But what about Keller?"

"That part you can help with," he said.

"Yeah?"

"Yeah. You two should go talk to that detective you met with. Wolmack, was it? I'm sure Detective Styles will want to hear about all this too."

I smiled and turned to look at Becky.

She laughed quietly. "Perfect."

We pulled up to the police station and walked inside. A young woman no older than thirty now sat at the front desk.

"Can I help you?" she asked.

"We are looking for Detective Wolmack ," I said.

"Oh, Wolmack. I think you just missed him."

"Do you know when he'll be back?"

She shook her head. "He got a break in some old case and brought in another detective from California, I think it was. They just went to see the family."

Aidan glanced at me then back to the woman.

"Was that the Callahan case by any chance?" he asked.

The woman shook her head. "I can't say. Can I take a message for you?"

"No. It's okay," he said. "We'll come back later. Thank you for your time."

He grasped my arm and led me quickly back to the car.

"Aidan, what's going on?"

"I'm pretty sure Wolmack is at Ethan's right now, and good money says Styles is with him."

"Why?"

"A break in an old case, right? And he brought in a detective from California?"

"Yeah, so?"

"That's just got to be Danny's case. I can feel it."

"Is that a bad thing?" Becky chirped.

"No," he said, "but I would rather him not tell Ethan anything yet."

"Why?"

"I just want to give Styles all the information we have first to avoid Ethan finding out too much."

"He's right," I said. "I don't want my dad knowing any details. I wouldn't want to know them myself if I had a choice."

Becky nodded. "Makes sense. Let's go."

Aidan sped down the wet roads to my house. We pulled up right as Wolmack and Styles were heading back to the car. It looked like Ethan was still at work, so we had gotten there in time. We got out of Aidan's car, and the detectives approached us. Instantly, I was assaulted with images from my past. I remembered him. He looked exactly the same save some gray at his temples. His face was round and childlike yet clearly showed his age. I thought I saw a strange expression cross his face when our eyes met, but it was gone so soon it left me wondering if it had ever really been there.

"We were just coming to talk to you," Styles said to me. "We have some good news."

"Let's go inside," Aidan said. "We have some things to tell you too."

He nodded, and we all headed back into the house.

We sat at the kitchen table, and Styles opened a case file.

"What did you find out?" I asked.

He exhaled softly before replying. "We found Daniel's body."

"What?" I bellowed. "Where?"

He put his hand up to stop me. "And dozens of others."

"Oh my God!"

"Daniel went missing after being sent to the morgue. There were dozens of bodies found buried in a lot here in Oregon."

"Why would they take Daniel back to California then back here to North Bend?" I asked.

"I wondered the same thing," he said. "I realized Daniel was killed here when our research led us to a possible underground religious sect—a cult perhaps. It appears they felt that the bodies needed to be returned to their home to be discovered by the police and then taken back to their precincts. It doesn't make sense, but nothing does in cases like this."

I nodded. "We have to talk…about a lot of things."

He nodded. "Did you know about this?"

Wolmack shifted in his seat and held his gaze on me.

I met his stare. "I told you we were going to try to solve Danny's case. We didn't want to say anything before we had proof. We have it now."

Wolmack sighed. "You should have let us handle this."

"I know. That is why we are telling you now. But you found Danny?" I asked, turning my attention back to Detective Styles. "And you are sure it's him?"

Styles nodded. "We're sure. And now, you can finally bury him properly."

I didn't realize I was crying until I felt Becky squeeze my shoulder. I leaned against her a little for some comfort. She didn't say anything, but I knew she was feeling the same kind of bittersweet emotion that I was. We could finally put my beloved brother to rest and get him some justice. We had Keller, and I knew that handing him over to the police was the right thing to do.

Chapter Eighteen

I WAS WEARING the only black dress I owned. I had never worn it before, but I figured this was as good a time as any. I stood beside Rudy and Becky with Ethan and my mom behind me. It was surreal, but I was aware enough for the pain to reach me. I cried softly as people spoke of their memories of Danny and shared childhood pictures. When it was my turn to speak, I gathered my courage and tried to keep myself together.

"I know we are supposed to be sad," I started, "because Daniel is gone. It is a sad thing to be without him, but I don't see it quite like that." I folded the paper that I had written the speech on, deciding not to read it. "I had written something, but I think what I have come to realize today is that there is something more important to say. Danny was an amazing person. He was a hero in more ways than one. He died fighting for the good he believed was still in this world. I see your tears, and I don't ignore my own, but maybe we should not be so sad. I will always miss him. We all will, but we're lucky too. We were blessed to have him in our lives even if it wasn't for as long as we would have liked. He was someone who brought out the best in us, brought out our love and our courage. He made us strong and always made us believe in ourselves. We are all better for knowing him, and that is how we will keep him alive."

I stepped down and returned to my seat. I started crying the second Becky grasped my hand.

After we said our goodbyes and laid my brother to rest, we returned home for a small memorial. We had one once before, but it wasn't the same. Now that Danny was home, we felt it right to have another.

My mom had flown out to be here. It was good to have her for support, but she wasn't handling it very well. She never talked about Danny. It was like she thought she could forget if she avoided the topic. I guess we had brought all of it back to the surface and opened old wounds. It was good, in a way, to feel the pain of missing him. In some way, the pain was another way I felt close to him. The happy memories and the sadness of missing him were all ways for me to stay connected. I wasn't like my mom; I didn't want to forget. I never wanted to forget.

The next day I was using to recover from all the mental depression and to let my body heal. Aidan was in my room, flipping through scrapbooks with me. I decided it was time to add him to the pages. It was time to stop trying to keep him away just to prove that I could. He was the one I wanted with me at all times. He was the one I always called out for when I was scared. I needed him in my life as much as he needed me. I knew that a life with him could never be normal, but it had been a long time since anything had been normal. Normality was not what I wanted anymore. I wanted Aidan—extraordinary, beautiful Aidan. Even if that meant that nothing would ever be normal, I knew—that it would be wonderful.

The morning was sunny, and the cast was finally off my leg. I was supposed to take it easy, to make sure it wouldn't swell up again. Becky and I were enjoying a normal cup of coffee at Books by the Bay.

"Are you okay?" she asked me.

I realized I was staring into my coffee. "Actually, I am," I said, looking up at her. "It seems like things have worked out."

She smiled. "I guess they have."

"It's going to take time," I told her. "A lot of time and a lot of support. I know I'll have some bad days, but I do believe that I can get through this and move on with my life."

"And move on with Aidan?" She batted her eyelashes playfully.

I laughed. "Yeah. That too."

"That's good. I hope you don't mind that I told Aaron."

"I don't. Just make sure he doesn't tell anyone else. I do hope you left out the details?"

She put her hand up. "Don't worry. I did exactly what Styles asked me to do. Nobody will know about the craziness that happened. I'm not sure who would believe it anyway."

I laughed. "Yeah, that's true."

I saw Aidan enter the café. He smiled at me and took the seat next to me.

"Hi," he sang as cheerful as ever.

"Hi," I answered, leaning in to kiss his cheek. He turned his head and met my lips unexpectedly. I pulled away, laughing.

"You two are too much," Becky said with a laugh.

"Am I interrupting?" he asked.

"Oh, yeah. We were just talking about you," Becky teased.

"Really?" he answered.

We both just smiled at him.

"Are you ready to go back to school?" he asked me.

"Oh God. Already?"

"Yeah," he said. "Your dad and I talked a little bit. He thinks you should stay home at least for the first few days. He was thinking about keeping you home all year and getting you a private tutor."

"Oh God." I laughed. "Please! Kill me now."

Becky giggled. "I think going to school would be a nice change."

"School makes me feel normal," I said. "At least let me have that."

Aidan smiled. "Sure. But are you positive you're ready?"

I nodded. "I'll be fine, Aidan. Thanks."

"Good," he said. "I hope we can move past this."

I nodded. "I already have. I will need your support, but I'm moving on."

He smiled at me. "I will always be here for you."

"There is something I wanted to ask you," I said, "something I have put a lot of thought into. I really think it would help if you could do just one small thing for me."

"What's that, Jane?"

I took a deep breath. "Aidan...I want to see the clearing."

Chapter Nineteen

I SAUNTERED FORWARD SLOWLY. I was barely even moving. Aidan turned around.

"Are you okay?"

I tried to smile but wasn't sure if I did. I followed him farther into the trees until we reached the clearing. I was assaulted by memories, as I expected, but this time, they didn't make me feel as sick. I half expected Sevren members to emerge like they had in the nightmare I had while at the compound. I looked to Aidan to calm my nerves and remind myself what was real.

The rocks were in the same place they had always been, and the old blood stains seemed to have faded.

"It seems like something from a dream."

Aidan put his arm around me, and I leaned into him.

"It never has to be more than a dream for you. We can both put it behind us."

I nodded softly against his shoulder. "I know we can. Together."

I felt him kiss my hair.

"Rudy wanted to thank you by the way," I said.

Aidan laughed. "Really? Rudy?"

I chuckled. "I guess he finally realizes you aren't the bad guy."

"About time."

I smiled. "It's good, you know."

He looked at me quizzically. "What is?"

"Everything. Even through all the pain and the suffering, I have you, Becky, Rudy, my parents. Danny is finally home where he belongs. I feel almost like I have some sense of…"

"Closure?"

I smirked. "Yeah. Exactly."

He grasped my hand, and I felt an almost electric shock surge through me. After all this time and everything we had been through, Aidan could still make me feel like I did the first time he ever touched me. It was definitely not normal, but it was good.

There was only a week left of summer, and Ethan was still trying to convince me to stay home at least for the first few days of school. He kept talking about "time to recover." I just wanted to put it behind me. I rejected every suggestion about therapy and every idea for what I should do to recover. I had all I needed in my friends. I was sure I would get some strange looks, and I expected people to talk. There were no secrets in North Bend, but none of that was new to me. I just had to stay focused on the good and move on with my life.

Acknowledgments

All of my thanks and appreciation go to my husband, the first person to read this book and my biggest fan. Thank you for always believing in me.

Special shout out to Annie-Belle, my Becky, for the trip to Oregon and the crazy antics that inspired this book.

Thank you to my editor, Kathy Moczerniak, for all your amazing help in making this book so much better than it was before. It would not have happened without you.

Special thanks to my family who always supported my passion and encouraged me to follow my dreams.

About the Author

Sara J Bernhardt is an author and poet who has been writing since a very young age and is a winner of several poetry and short story contests. She lives in Southern California with her husband and cat. It is clear that Bernhardt writes in a realistic tone while still creating the enthralling feeling of fantasy. Her writing puts readers in a world that they will truly love to be a part of.

You can follow Sara at these locations:

Facebook: www.facebook.com/Sara-J-Bernhardt
Amazon: www.amazon.com/Sara-J.-Bernhardt
Website: www.sjbernhardt.com

Also by SARA J. BERNHARDT

https://www.amazon.com/Sara-J.-Bernhardt/e/B07DNFCH5J/

Summer's Deceit (Hunters Trilogy – Book 1): Jane Callahan is a reclusive, seventeen-year-old high school student dealing with the death of her beloved brother. Her home in Southern California with her mother is a constant reminder of her loss and pain. In hopes of escaping her past she moves to North Bend Oregon to live with her father, where she meets a beautiful boy named Aidan Summers. Jane is intrigued by his looks as well as his unusual ways of attempting to get her attention. After months of uncommon conversation and frustration, an uncertain romance brews between Jane and Aidan, but Aidan has a ghastly secret that could destroy everything.

Summer's Shadow (Hunters Trilogy – Book 2): Aidan Summers, a seventeen-year-old, stunningly beautiful genius, somehow finds his way into the life of Jane Callahan; a lovely girl trapped in soggy North Bend, Oregon. In this new Tale by Sara J. Bernhardt, Aidan relates his side of the story. All of his dark secrets are revealed and all of his motivations behind his strange ways become known as the story unravels in a captivating narrative of suspense, romance, courage...and murder.

Summer's Redemption (Hunters Trilogy – Book 3): The secret alliance of The Silver Wing and the waging war with their evil rival, The Sevren, come into full view in a new light. The evil that still lurks and stirs behind the supposed destruction of The Sevren steps out of the shadows and spins a new tale of adventure, suspense, romance, mystery and terror.

Behind Blue Eyes Series

A father's desire to save his child presents him with an unthinkable choice that leaves him darker than human, forced to roam through time alone as he searches for the place he belongs.

Adam Gold – Book 1: Fleeing the French invasion of Geneva Switzerland in the 1700s, Adam Gold books passage to America with his family. On the ship, Adam's daughter falls fatally ill. A mysterious man comes to Adam with a way to save his child by turning Adam into something darker than human.

The Medallion – Book 2: Adam Gold, an immortal with sweet eyes of blue, rushes through the centuries on a quest for reason and a thirst for revenge. To cope with his pain and regret, he sleeps away the years and awakes in a new era with a powerful, ancient vampire who sets her sights on him.

Golden Shackles – Book 3: When the ancient queen, Sekhmet snatches up Adam, he is faced with a terrifying decision. To help aid her in her vile plans or dare to stand against her.

Plus 3 more segments!

In Gray

After a near fatal car crash brings Daisy Carmichael the ability to see the future, she is plagued by not only the things she sees, but the deadly secrets of the boy who saved her life.

Also from the Lavish Publishing family

Sinister Series
A. Nicky Hjort
https://www.lavishpublishing.com/authors/nicky-hjort-1/

Thrillers that will take you to the edge and leave you breathless! Mature adult reads due to graphic sexual and violent material...

Sinister Bouquet: Awakening - Book 1: Devyn Mitchell has a choice... listen to the voice of her unborn baby – or die- again.

After a near death experience, Doctor Devyn Mitchell finds herself not only mysteriously pregnant but able to communicate with her fetus.

She has two choices: give in to total madness or surrender to her new reality, which just may be the only way she and her family will survive the obsessions of the Homeless Hunter's mind.

A true paranormal romantic thriller, A Sinister Bouquet: Awakening, the first of the Sinister Series, will take you right to the edge of what you know to be possible and then drop you in a place so dark, so terrifying, that the only passageway out is through the blinding light of awakening.

Wake up.
   Open your eyes.
   Finally.
   We've missed you so.

Sinister Vision: Know This Much Is True – Book 2: Elise Phillips, a doctor in training, has successfully repressed her kidnapping five years prior.

The only problem is...she has six and one half days to remember every terrible detail, or a total stranger will die. But to make matters even worse, in order to save this nameless woman, Elise will have to face something that scares her even more than death–intimacy.

Another paranormal romantic thriller, A Sinister Vision: Know This Much is True, the second of the Sinister Series, will take you even further over the edge of what you know to be possible and guide you right back out through the only way left...impossible.

Wake up. Open your eyes. Accept your assignment.
   ...The problem is not to find the answer–but to face it.

Know this much is true.

Fairfield Corners Series
L.A. Remenicky
http://myBook.to/FairfieldCorners

Small town romance with a paranormal twist! Each in standalone style, read and enjoy any order, any number!

Saving Cassie – Book 1: Some secrets are too dangerous to keep.

After ten years in the big city, Cassie Holt is back in Fairfield Corners. She may look like the same girl who left home a decade before but she's hiding a dark truth from everyone. When her life is threatened by the demons of her past, her best friend—who happens to be the local sheriff—offers his help.

Deputy Logan Miller has been burned by love. He's not looking to get involved but duty calls when the sheriff tasks him with Cassie's protection. Thrown into close quarters with the gorgeous bookseller, sparks fly. Logan is drawn to Cassie, but it's hard to get close to someone who keeps themselves guarded all the time.

To keep Cassie safe, Logan must open his heart but that's something he swore he'd never do.

Ragan's Song – Book 2: One look into his eyes told her she was in trouble – again!

Ragan returned home to celebrate her parent's anniversary hoping they would forgive her the secrets she's kept from them over the last few years. When she discovered that Adam was still living in Fairfield Corners she hoped her secrets were safe, secrets that drove her away three years, secrets that could change both their lives forever.

Adam Bricklin was devastated when Ragan Newlin left town. No note, no email, no text. She was just gone. It has taken three years for Adam to finally move past the heartbreak he suffered when Ragan left town. Now he's moved on and everything was going well until the day Ragan returned to Fairfield Corners. Now the melody that he lost all those years ago is back. It's the same tune he heard that tells him right from wrong—the one that sang Ragan was the one.

Even separation can't silence Adam and Ragan's song, and now that she's back it's time for Adam to decide if he should let the song die or breathe life into it once again.

Where There's Faith – Book 3: A past she can't remember. A love he can't forget.

After losing everything in an accident that he can only blame himself for, Robbie Newlin embraced sobriety and tried to live his life quietly alone at this family's cottage on the lake. Grief being his only ally, Robbie was perfectly content with how he lived until Faith moved into the cottage next door. Now Faith had him questioning whether to keep grieving or to open his broken heart to let love in again.

Faith McMillan had no memory of her life before that day three years ago. The physical scars had faded but the emotional ones were still fresh and raw. Living rent-free seemed like a great way to finish her second book and give her the time to figure out her next move, but then she met the reclusive guy next door and everything changed.

To get past the broken parts, Robbie and Faith must figure out if they want to continue living their lives in solitude or take a chance on finding an ending together.

www.ingramcontent.com/pod-product-compliance
Lightning Source LLC
Chambersburg PA
CBHW061231170626
46809CB00007B/2616